Bishop Putnam

American patriotism; an essay

Bishop Putnam

American patriotism; an essay

ISBN/EAN: 9783337305635

Printed in Europe, USA, Canada, Australia, Japan

Cover: Foto ©Andreas Hilbeck / pixelio.de

More available books at **www.hansebooks.com**

AMERICAN PATRIOTISM

AN ESSAY

BY

PUTNAM P. BISHOP

AUTHOR OF "THE PSYCHOLOGIST"

———

NEW YORK & LONDON

G. P. PUTNAM'S SONS

The Knickerbocker Press

1887

Press of
G. P. Putnam's Sons
New York

CONTENTS.

AMERICAN PATRIOTISM.

GENESIS AND GROWTH.

Patriotism has been so mighty a factor in the history of the world, that we naturally regard it as having been ordained from above. Moreover, for one who is inclined to study the mental constitution of man, it is easy to see that the evolution of this affection is assured by structural necessity. Its fountain head, in common with the primary source of love of kindred, love of party and several other affections, is what I have elsewhere called "Susceptibility to Consciousness of Ownership." I mean by "Ownership" the relation denoted by the possessive pronouns. When I am so related to any object of contemplation, be it a person, a class of persons, an organization, or an aggregate, however simple or multifarious in its component parts, that I call it "mine,"—the apprehension of that relation is a cause of delight to me, and that delight becomes inseparably associated in my mind with the object contemplated. Then, under an immutable law of my nature, my heart re-acts in affection toward the object which is occupying my thoughts when that special enjoyment is experienced.

It is evident that the emergence of patriotism in the young heart presupposes the intellectual conception of a country distinguished from all other countries, and the apprehension of this distinctive relation to it. Hence, the growth and character of the affection depend very largely on intellectual development. The conception may come far short of embracing all the territory and population subject to a common government. A clan, a tribe or a race, with the limited area inhabited by it, or a section whose people have exclusive interests and traditions in common, may completely fill out the mental picture of one's country and, in this case, the reach of the affection will be correspondingly restricted. Still in all such cases we have a territory and a population to which the individual is joyously conscious of a possessory relation ; and the structurally necessitated affection which responds to this consciousness, is identical in origin and essence with full-grown and comprehensive patriotism.

This affection, in common with all others which inevitably come into being in the progress of mental evolution, is strengthened by various forces which proceed from other points in our spiritual nature. One after another, trains of association connect themselves with the conception of our country, and, thenceforward, elicit keen delight from our inborn susceptibilities. Our hearts respond with an accession of love to the interest with which we dwell on the events of our national history. When we contemplate the hardships experienced by our forefathers, we place to the credit of our country both our own delightful consciousness of the worthiness of our sympathies, and the fortitude and high principles with which those hardships were encountered. We bless our country for the heart-thrills which attend our remembrance of the sages and heroes of the revolutionary period; and we feel that we have a proprietary interest in the self-sacrificing spirit and all the high virtues displayed by "the generation of '76." Thoughts of the unparalleled growth of our country awaken an exultant joy, but little short of that which we could derive from the swiftest advancement of our personal fortunes. Even that awful struggle which, but a few years ago, was filling our hearts with torture, and causing them to react in fiery passion, is already yielding in rich abundance the fruits on which patriotism feeds and thrives. We rejoice in the demonstration of the universal readiness of American citizens to die for their convictions; and our country stands before us clothed in all the heroism which characterized the opposing hosts. We see the one " root of bitterness " in our national institutions annihilated, and the remembrance of fratricidal strife is now sweetening our thoughts of the internal peace which shall never end. When we rise to a higher plane, and take a more comprehensive view, and breathe the atmosphere of " good-will toward men," our hearts are made to swell with a "joy unspeakable" by the reflection, that it is OUR country that has been chosen for an agency of measureless beneficence—OUR country that has demonstrated the compatibility of Liberty with Order—OUR country that has repudiated all hereditary mastery, and guaranteed " equality of opportunity" to all citizens—OUR country that has solved the problem of combining local self-government with national unity and national sovereignty—OUR country whose self-governing States are annually pouring out their millions in the cause of universal enlightenment—OUR country that bids all Christian organizations an impartial "God-speed," and promises that no one of them shall work at a disadvantage in appealing to the understandings and consciences of men. Under the laws of our nature the delights which come to us from all these sources, redound to the strengthening and intensification of our patriotism.

It is interesting to trace the

MARKS OF CREATIVE WISDOM AND BENEVOLENCE

in all these structurally necessitated impulses. That the welfare of each individual may be made possible, Man is so constituted that an indestructible desire of enduring happiness emerges so soon as the idea of personal existence as a whole becomes distinct. That the helpless may receive due care, and that there may be mutual helpfulness in the family circle, the origination of parental affection and of the more comprehensive love of kindred, is provided for in Susceptibility to Consciousness of Ownership. That each member of a community may be incited to promote the welfare of all its other members, it is ordained that each shall have a sense of proprietary interest in the community to which he belongs. That the citizens of a particular State may exert themselves for those public interests with which they are most familiar, and which they are best able to promote, each of them has in his susceptibility to Consciousness of Ownership a fountain which only selfishness can keep from yielding an ardent love for the State of his birth or his adoption. Thus it is provided that, as our mental powers are unfolded, and more extended relations come into view, love to the smaller aggregate shall reach out and embrace the larger aggregate, until its maturity and consummation shall be realized in that patriotism which is the most comprehensive affection originated in the susceptibility that I have named.

All these affections, alike, are designed to subserve the divine good-will to mankind ; and, if they were never perverted through ignorance

and selfishness, there could be no conflict among
them. It is best for the individual to cultivate
an operative, self-sacrificing love for his kindred, his community, his State and his country. The true welfare of a family is bound up
in the welfare of the community in which it is
embodied. It is unwise in a community to attempt its own advancement at the expense of
principles which are salutary to the State of
which it forms a part. Most assuredly, the
well-being of a State, in its most important as-
pects, is conditioned on the observance of those
constitutional limitations, and the adoption of
those governmental measures which are best
for the nation at large. We see, therefore, that,
while provision is made for the special beneficence of each individual within the sphere of
which he has completest knowledge, and which
offers him the most numerous opportunities, it
is designed, also, that, as he becomes capable
of broader surveys, his love shall go forth to
larger aggregates, and that he shall rise at length
to a consciousness of identification with an aggregate which includes all the others, and see
that every act promotive of the welfare of his
country is an act of beneficence toward all

the objects of his less comprehensive affections.

It is unnecessary to adduce arguments in support of the proposition, that a moral obligation connects itself with each of the impulses which spring of necessity from the constitution of our mental nature. We all accept that view. If a man's passions keep him from displaying an intelligent regard for his own welfare, we call him "a fool," whatever may be his intellectual gifts. A man "without natural affection," is an object of abhorrence to us. A citizen destitute of public spirit is regarded with universal disfavor; and a man whose selfishness smothers all regard for the welfare of his State or his country, finds no defenders. Thus, however few may have formulated the doctrine to themselves, all men assume that human worthiness is measured by conformity to the creative design which manifests itself in the structure of the human soul.

We see this truth illustrated still farther when we consider that intelligent patriotism, within its sphere, coincides perfectly with intelligent philanthrophy. The evolution of this latter impulse is necessitated by an original Susceptibility to Perception of Happiness. In early life, before any considerable growth of distorting and corrupting passions can have taken place, the external signs of happiness are agreeable, while the external signs of un-happiness are painful, to all human beings. The natures of very few persons ever become so perverted that joy-expressing smiles are not more pleasing to them than the lines of sorrow upon a human countenance. It is provided that, through this susceptibility, and that ac-quisitive impulse, which is the common charac-teristic of all desires, and which calls for the prevalence of that which gives us pleasure, we shall wish for the welfare of mankind so far as it is an object of contemplation to us. It is true that we cannot expect to find philanthropy, as an operative force, coupled with an intellect scarcely able to form the conception of man-kind at large; true that the growth of selfish-ness in the heart of man involves the growth of indifference to human welfare in general, and true that the rise of malignant passions, di-rectly antagonistic to far-reaching benevolence, is among the possibilities of human nature.

Still, it remains unquestionable that provisions for the evolution of philanthropy are among the marks of creative design plainly observable in our mental constitution; and no one will deny that "Good-will toward men" is a chief element of human worthiness.

We get a clearer view of the high rank which patriotism is designed to occupy among our possible virtues, when we consider that it is necessarily re-enforced by all our philanthropic impulses. Whatever good we see to be an element of human welfare, and crave for our race, becomes an object of still more fervent desire in behalf of the growing millions of our fellow-countrymen. If we contemplate beneficent agencies promising enlightenment and elevation to the world, and are moved to contribute to their force, that impulse is mightily strengthened when our country comes into view, presenting her special claims upon us, and offering us the sphere wherein our exertions can be most effective.

As Americans, we hear with especial distinctness the authoritative voice of philanthropy demanding the cultivation of patriotism. In so far as we love our race, we desire that upward paths may lie open to all men; that hereditary distinctions may everywhere cease to maintain barriers between merit and reward; that the completest personal liberty compatible with public safety may be enjoyed throughout the world; that a sense of responsibility for governmental action may foster self-respect in every man; that every man may see in universal education a measure of safety for himself and his posterity, and that governments may everywhere recognize the equal rights of all religious organizations. I need not say that the realization of all these ends will, of necessity, be hastened or delayed by the events which are to be embodied in the future history of the United States. Many leaders of opinion still deny that our institutions have passed beyond the experimental stage; and it is safest for us to assume the justice of that view. Then we shall take something like an adequate measure of the responsibility of American citizens for the general welfare of mankind. Let us remember that our country is as "a city set upon a hill," and that nothing of moment can be "done in a corner" within her borders. The fruits of self-government in the United States will inevitably evoke either a paralyzing distrust of all such institutions as ours, or kindle fervent aspirations prophetic of personal freedom and "equality of opportunity" in other lands.

It will occur to every thoughtful person that no one can enjoy the blessings with which American citizenship is fraught, and still take little interest in the welfare of his country, without base ingratitude. It is only the heart possessed by sordid selfishness, which can fail to respond with operative and ever-ready love in view of such boons as our country vouchsafes to us. Here, also, we find the stimulation of patriotism comprehended in the creative design.

We have seen that all our structurally necessitated impulses which have human welfare for their object, from the desire of personal happiness up to the most comprehensive affection of which we are capable, operate legitimately toward the invigoration of our patriotism. Still another consideration,—and one of immeasureable moment,—is pertinent at this point. The dissociation of moral obligation from human power is an impossible occurrence. Ability to act upon the world, however restricted or extended, brings with it the duty to act beneficently. The American voter, by reason of the simple fact that he is empowered to cast a ballot, is divinely called upon to watch and work for the welfare of America. None of us, without being false to Duty, can abstain from exerting, or can exert heedlessly, the influence whereby the future of our country may be affected.

We now pass to the consideration of

THE FRUITS OF PATRIOTISM.

Self-sacrifice in warfare is the manifestation of the affection which has received most attention and oftenest afforded the themes with which poets and orators have kindled our imaginations and stirred our hearts. It is creditable to our nature that we are susceptible to such appeals, and that it is only a very low stage of degradation that is marked by the possibility of contemplating with indifference the soldier's readiness to die for his country. Yet it is evident that this is not the form of patriotism which is most difficult of attainment. Every impulse of the human heart is called into more vehement activity by opposition. Danger to an object of affection stimulates love to put forth the fullness of its power. Real or imagined wrong to an object of affection arouses that indignation,—that impulse to punish,—which over-matches all other springs of action in energizing force. It is easy to see, therefore, that a patriotism, which is nearly dormant in periods of national tranquillity, may be heated by the fires of war to such fervor that all counting of personal cost will seem contemptible. When we consider, also, the prevalence of intelligence in our land, and the consequent general understanding of such reasons for the cultivation of patriotism as I have mentioned, we have no ground for apprehending that any future conflict will find Americans unwilling to offer themselves in defence of their country.

But occasions for such outbursts of American patriotism are to be classed among improbable events. Public opinion, throughout the civilized world, is rapidly becoming conscientious. It is beginning to apply the standard of rectitude to the proceedings of nations, as well as to those of individuals. Ability to crush an adversary is no longer regarded as justification of war. National aggrandizement alone is no longer held to be a legitimate object of national aggression. It is already certain that the American people will never sanction a declaration of war in opposition to the manifest demands of justice; and, as the morality inculcated by Jesus of Nazareth makes its way among the nations of the earth, and ruling classes become convinced of the prudence of deferring to the convictions of those whom they rule, the probability of bloody strife between Bible-reading peoples becomes more and more remote. For these reasons, and because of our freedom from entangling alliances, we have ever enlarging grounds to hope for the peaceful adjustment of any complications which may arise between other countries and our own.

But just because American patriotism is not likely to be converted into an all-controlling passion by an out-break of war, there is all the more need of its deliberate, systematic and persistent cultivation by thoughtful Americans. In the absence of external stimuli our virtues will decay unless they have a basis in steadfast principle founded on conviction. We should remember that bloodshed is not the greatest calamity that can befall a nation, and that unrighteousness will continue to war against welfare in all aggregates of human beings. As it is only by constant struggling that the individual can save himself from degeneration, so it is only through the watchful and laborious patriotism of her sons, that a country can be assured immunity from the growth of abuses prolific of wretchedness. The downward gravitation of men, and of all aggregates of men, should never be forgotten.

It is obvious that the channels through which patriotism can legitimately pour its benign influences are numberless. We will confine ourselves, however, to considerations connected with

THE RIGHT OF SUFFRAGE.

Patriotic Americans competent to an intelligent survey of the public needs, and capable of tracing causes to their effects, must see very clearly that their responsibility is greatly increased by the certainty that large masses of their fellow-citizens will vote ignorantly, and that other masses of them are sure to vote selfishly. Enormous volumes of power, having no connection with intelligent regard for the public welfare, are to make themselves felt in public affairs. This evil is greatly aggravated by the ease with which the unprincipled can control the ignorant. Men of the latter class are exposed on all sides to such artifices as honest men never employ. The demagogue revels in lies, and knows how to create an insatiable appetite for lies. His promises of special benefits to his hearers are adjusted to his conception of the extent of their gullibility. But his chief resource is the stirring up of animosities against those whom he desires to overcome at the ballot-box ; for it is unfortunately true that hatred is evoked by the merest touch upon susceptibilities pervaded by selfishness and subject to no conscientious regulation. When this man is followed by one who has chosen truth for his companion, who sees ignominy in all deceptive arts and detects the atmosphere of hell in all appeals to evil passions, the best that it seems possible to hope for is the evidence of impregnable stupidity. It happens, upon occasions that the demagogue's aims are coincident at certain points with the demands of public welfare. But it is none the less true that evil to the public is inseparable from the arts which he employs, and that corrupting influences swell

and expand at each stage in his personal success. It is for the right-minded American citizen to find in these things an ever-present
menace to his country, and a call to renewed
vigilance and more arduous exertion.

But patriotism, like all other human affections, is liable to be misguided. An operative
impulse toward a given end does not always
bear assurance that the end will be promoted.
The working of harm by efforts designed to be
helpful is a matter of every day occurrence. Mistakes in the diagnosis of evils are sure to be followed by mistakes in the application of reme-
dies. Moreover, when the evils to be cured
and the needs to be supplied are clearly appre-
hended, a consequence far worse than mere
failure often ensues by reason of erroneous judgment concerning the suitableness of the means
employed to the ends which are held in view.
In public affairs especially, so many forces are
at work and so many lines of causation are to
be taken into account, that the danger of bringing about results directly opposite to those
which are intended is immense. These considerations make it plain that the first duty of the
patriot connects itself with his own intelligence.

It is only through the apprehension of truth that the external beneficence of a worthy affection can be assured.

That it is the American citizen's duty to acquaint himself with public affairs as fully as his circumstances permit, is too obvious for argument. We have no right to neglect obtainable light in taking action which must affect our fellow-men. Neither have we a right to "bury in a napkin" a power which we can qualify ourselves to employ usefully. But we should bear in mind that the mere gathering of information is but the beginning of adequate equipment for the duties associated with the right of suffrage. The cultivation of that skill in tracing causes to their effects, and in discerning the suitableness or unsuitableness of means to ends, which is of the essence of all practical wisdom, is equally obligatory upon us. Finally, that our duty to our country requires us to guard the integrity of our understandings against the assaults, not only of passion and prejudice, but, also, of our predilections and dislikes, no thoughtful person can fail to see.

Viewed in this light, does the yoke of American patriotism appear heavy? Are we so blind that we cannot see in each of these obligations an invitation to "go up higher" in the scale of being? To my own mind, our country presents the divinest feature of her mission when she calls upon her children, in the name of their filial love, to clothe themselves with personal excellence. But an immutable law makes endeavor the price of permanent good; and the values of possible boons are proportioned to the arduousness of the struggles through which they may be gained. Hence, the very fact, that the growth of enlightened patriotism involves a large increase of personal worthiness, sufficiently evidences that the cultivation of the affection is fraught with many difficulties. That some of these may be seen more clearly, I will point out

Three Vices Antagonistic to Patriotism.

I have heard it said that a preacher is most effective when he is most fully conscious of his own faults, and preaches to himself as well as to his congregation. If this is true, what I have to say upon these vices should not be wholly destitute of force; for I have never succeeded in keeping myself entirely free from them, but have always found that a suspension of watchfulness was sure to bring me under their power:

1. *Intellectual Laziness.*

Laziness in general is apt to be spoken of contemptuously. It is not often, however, that we take an adequate measure of its essential viciousness. When we see it apparently occasioning loss only to the lazy person himself, our contempt is of that good-natured variety which is entirely compatible with warm friendship. It is only when it causes the disregard of weighty responsibilities, that it excites our indignation. But, if we care to trace it to its origin, we come by a single step upon that same tendency to self-indulgence which is the fountain-head of all human iniquity. A man is distinguished from the lower animals in so far as he is not an automaton, and is not controlled by his spontaneous dispositions and disinclinations, but fixes his aims on those high and remote objects which commend themselves to his reason, and seeks the fulfillment of his mission in self-coercion. Hence, at the very beginning of that continuous struggle which is made the price of human welfare, he encounters within himself a disinclination to all activities which are not spontaneous. In the fact, that self-coercion is an indispensable condition of well-being, we find what men have called "Depravity," and laziness would seem to be its first-born offspring. I have tried to keep myself apart from those who concentrate their thoughts upon a particular vice, and get in the way of ascribing to it nearly all the ills which deface the condition of mankind. But it is easy to see that a general habit of self-indulgence may originate in laziness, and that men often abandon themselves to evil tendencies because of disinclination to the exertions which repression would cost.

It is in keeping with the creative regulation under which the requirement of exertion is proportioned to the value of the boon which is sought, that disinclination to exertion bears more severely upon our higher powers than upon our lower powers. Hence intellectual laziness is both more common and more pernicious than physical laziness. We should remember that the presence of this vice is entirely compatible with great intellectual activity. As a young man may be always ready for a game of base-ball, but never ready to earn his dinner by sawing wood, so one's faculties may obey spontaneous impulses with extreme vivacity and yet betray an invincible sluggishness when a sense of duty is pressing upon them. In a thousand ways intellectual vivacity may be actually hostile to that power for the ascertainment of truth which it is the patriot's duty to cultivate. Ability to produce effects of a given class may have an enormous growth at the expense of one's understanding. Even a thirst for knowledge may serve to disqualify one for the duties of American citizenship. In all these cases there is a demand for that self-coercion the absence of which is a manifestation of laziness. We see, therefore, that this vice is always threatening to misguide our patriotism, and that it is only by ceaseless vigilance and by resolute and persistent endeavor, that we can fully equip ourselves for the high post of an American voter.

The extent of the needful self-coercion will become clearer to us as we consider the prevalence and power of another vice :

2. *Aversion to Corrective Light.*

When we have adopted views and conceptions so fully that they have become incorporated in our mental nature, we dislike to have
them disturbed. Because, for the time being,
they are a part of us, any in-coming of light,
which seems to reveal unsoundness in them, we
feel to be an assault upon ourselves. In proportion as they have caused us to credit ourselves with the possession of truth, they have
become cherished objects to us, and we resent
any attack upon them as an attempt to rob us
of treasures. When the in-flow of corrective
light tends to unsettle convictions which have
served as starting-points for our generalizations,
and entered largely into our conclusions, it
seems to us that we are threatened with something like the total demolition of our intellectual world. But the keenest annoyance is
felt and the strongest impulse to resistance is
awakened when the opinions disturbed are associated with ardent affections. An unfavorable
light upon the object of our love, as well as a
favorable light on the object of our hatred, is
exceedingly offensive. To make the matter
worse, we are apt to hear an insidious vanity

saying to us: "If you permit your opinion to be changed, you will acknowledge that you have been a fool."

Perhaps I am exceptionally weak at this point of my nature. However that may be, I frankly confess that the correction of my opinions is very disagreeable to me. I have been aware for many years that this fact is discreditable. I have seen very clearly that, if I were what I ought to be, all light enabling me to exchange error for truth would be most welcome, and that the modification of opinions is inseparable from growth in wisdom. Still, it remains true that I am apt to get angry whenever truth conflicting with my cherished convictions is forced upon me. The fair-minded investigation of a subject on which I have intense feeling, is very hard for me. I am disinclined to read a treatise, or listen to a discourse, in which my views are controverted. When I have deep feeling on matters requiring me to take action, I understand clearly that it is only through arduous self-coercion that I can qualify myself completely for the discharge of my duty.

Though others may be more fortunate than I am in respect to constitutional tendencies,

observation convinces me that the vice of which
I am speaking is widely prevalent. I find that
very few persons evince a teachable spirit when
they are offered facts and arguments adverse to
their favorite theories in philosophy, science,
religion or politics. How many persons in
every thousand read impartially what is said
on both sides of controverted questions in
which they take a deep interest? In how large
a proportion of American homes can one find
in equal abundance the documents issued by
opposing political parties? How often does
an ardent member of one party attend a meet-
ing of the opposite party in order to gain instruction? It cannot be denied that, as a rule,
the chief object of American citizens, in giving attention to political discussion, is the confirmation of opinions which they already entertain. The distastefulness of corrective light
involves, of course, the agreeableness of confirming light, and, in most men who have
decided convictions on matters of public interest, the appetite for confirmation is very
strong, while in many of us it has the energy
of a passion.

One may witness some very striking exhi-

bitions of repugnance to such' truth as tends
to disturb inveterate conceptions. To be dis-
pleased by truth which bears against those
whom we love, is a fault which " leans to virtue's side." But I have seen very religious men,
who had no doubt of the sureness of their " calling and election," grow white with anger at a
statement of facts which cast a favorable light
upon a class of their fellow-citizens. The corrective light, not only disturbed their conceptions, but also convicted them of unjustifiable ill-will; and the resentment, which re-
sponded to their remorse, was strong enough
to confirm their unjust belief and re-enforce
their hatred. Most assuredly, a vice which can
bear such fruits as these, is a vice against which
we cannot guard ourselves too vigilantly.

A majority of American voters rely on the
partisan press for political instruction ; and
their repugnance to correction unites with their
love of confirmation to confine them almost
exclusively to the newspapers which support
their own party. To what extent is the voter
qualified, in this way, for the exercise of enlightened patriotism ? There is no safety in
hasty generalizations upon this subject—no

reasonableness in sweeping statements. What is true in respect to some partisan newspapers is entirely false as to others. To say that, on the whole, the influence of the partisan press is pernicious, or even to say that it is valueless, would be very far from the truth. At the worst, it furnishes a knowledge of some facts which must be understood before one can vote intelligently; and its expositions of the bearings of those facts, however one-sided or bungling, is apt to stimulate the reader of ordinary intelligence to independent reflection. Moreover, among the men engaged in writing partisan editorials, we may find those, here and there, who are cultivated, fair-minded, sincerely patriotic and well equipped in all ways for the bestowment of political instruction. Almost of necessity, however, they are *advocates.* They seldom even profess to discuss political issues in a judicial frame of mind; and, if we read upon their side alone, we are in the condition of a juryman whom we may suppose to listen attentively to the plaintiff's counsel, but to keep his fingers in his ears while being addressed by the counsel for the defense. But the actual condition is very far from what it

would be if all editors endeavored to be true to
their mission as public teachers. They are
human beings like the rest of us, and peculiar
temptations are incident to their vocation as
well as to every other course of life on which
a man can enter. They are equally liable with
other men to prove intellectually lazy and
averse to corrective light; and the instances
are not rare in which they lack the natural
capacity and breadth of intelligence which
necessarily enter into qualifications for salutary guidance. The powers of many of them
are largely engrossed in efforts to save their
establishments from insolvency; and in some
of the more prosperous editors avarice "grows
by what it feeds upon," and duty to the public
is subordinated to the increase of circulation and
advertising patronage. When falsehood is seen
to be more acceptable than truth to a considerable class of readers, falsehood is uttered.
If fostering prejudices and pandering to animosities are believed to be conditions of an
increased demand for the paper, the price is
paid without hesitation. What measures shall
be commended depends entirely on what is supposed to be the general wish of the class of

readers chiefly relied on for patronage. As
the growth of personal selfishness always yields
an exaggerated conception of the general baseness of society, the moral tone of such a jour-
nal sinks even below the level on which avarice
would be surest of its objects. I am convinced,
however, that journalism of this description is
steadily losing ground; for I observe a steady
increase in the number of journalists who find
no difficulty in harmonizing the high responsibilities of their position with such reasonable
guardianship of personal interests as is incum-
bent upon all men. Nevertheless, the influence
of editorial work completely subordinated to
conscienceless money-making must be taken
into account, if we would comprehend the misguidance of American voters whom aversion
to corrective light makes dependent on a single
partisan newspaper for political instruction.

There are journals of other classes by which
we are in equal danger of being misled. There
are editors of great natural abilities and fine
attainments, whom passion has made utterly incapable of candor. They have already brought
on themselves the culminating punishment,
"that seeing they may see not, neither under-

stand." They can view in its true light no single fact pertaining to political issues, or bearing on the respective merits of opposing candidates. Literally and thoroughly, they have "made fools of themselves." Amid the wretched distortions which fill the intellectual medium created by their passions, they fancy that they are animated by a glowing zeal for righteousness, while they are pouring out denunciations of the upright and heaping encomiums on the base. When we think, also, of the editors who are self-consciously indifferent to truth; the editors who are wholly devoted to the promotion of special interests, regardless of the general welfare, and the editors who sink all manliness in the service of personal organs, we cannot fail to see that self-restriction to a single journalistic source of political information is unpatriotic, and that we must discipline ourselves to reach out in all directions for instruction on public affairs if we would be true to our country. Whatever expenditure of will-power the effort may cost us, we must seek illumination, whether it be corrective light or confirming light that is brought within our reach.

3. *Partisan Servility.*

Every vice originates in the perversion of
impulses whose legitimate activities are productive of virtue. The original susceptibility
which gives birth to love of party is the same
that I have pointed out as the fountain-head
of patriotism. It follows that love of party,
or party spirit, or partisanship, whichever name
one may choose to employ, is a worthy affection when it is kept under fit regulation. It is
then a mighty stimulant to exertion designed
to be beneficent. Its appointed instrumentality is truth; and its principal legitimate
office is the promulgation of such truth as tends
to strengthen the party that is loved and to
weaken the opposite party. As the ends of
justice are promoted by the arguments of opposing advocates on the evidence submitted
in a given case, so the presentation of truths
bearing in favor of each party, and of truths
bearing against each party, subserves the ends
.of patriotism so far as attention is given in a
truth-seeking spirit. When party spirit moves
men in official stations to strengthen their party
by endowing it with the credit of salutary
measures, it displays a beneficence of exalted

character. When combined with enlightened patriotism, "good-will toward men," and loyalty to the Right, partisanship is a force of such benign potency, that we have reason to thank our Creator for having made us capable of it.

But, as desire of needful food may pass over into gluttony, and as regard for the well-being of one's family may give birth to avarice, so party spirit may degenerate into partisan servility. At the very beginning of such a descent in the scale of being, the understanding is enslaved. Our desire to think well of the party we love is permitted to become so unduly powerful, that we are made disloyal to truth. We are impelled to the indiscriminate defence of the leaders of our party, of the measures embodied in its history, and of all the features of the policy which it proclaims. That we may be armed for this warfare, we eagerly seize on all facts that can be made, by any ingenuity in distortion, to cast a light encouraging to our passion, while we angrily repel from the sphere of our mental vision such facts as have an opposite bearing. Then aversion to corrective light comes in to double the weight of the chains in which our understandings are bound;

and, thenceforward, the two vices incessantly feed and pamper each other. The same force which, in a time of war, makes a self-sacrificing patriot of a citizen who cares little for his country in a time of peace, is sure to make partisan servility more blind and passionate. At frequently recurring periods, the servile partisan apprehends that the party which he loves is in danger of being overthrown by the party which he hates; and all considerations in favor of tranquil reasoning are thrown to the winds. Even the admonitions of conscience are perverted to the aggravation of his enslavement. He cannot wholly blind himself to the unworthiness of his passion. He cannot avoid seeing that there is personal degradation and absence of patriotism in abstaining from the candid investigation of matters which concern the welfare of his country; nor can he keep himself in ignorance of the fact that unveracity enters largely into the clamors which he is helping to raise against his political adversaries. But he associates the remorse which he experiences with the party against which he is battling, and thus his hatred is intensified and the blindness of his understanding is deepened. He illustrates the ease with which a paternal warning from heaven can be transformed into a seductive invitation from hell.

Of course partisan servility, like every other vice and like all virtues, is a subject of gradation. In the government of political and official action it exerts all degrees of force, from the creation of a bias which affects the judgment but slightly to the maintenance of an absolute despotism which, so far as political matters are concerned, is utterly destructive of the right to be classed among rational beings. It is probable that none of us who care much for politics are entirely free from the vice. For my own part, most certainly, I dare not assert that party-spirit never operates viciously upon my understanding; and when I examine the utterances and observe the actions of our statesmen, I am unable, on this score, to credit the most candid of them with more than I claim for myself. A reader of the Congressional Record will not fail to be impressed with the plentifulness of partisan tirades. Connecting-points for such outbursts are found in subjects which have no conceivable bearing on the comparative merits of parties. There are able men

in both houses of Congress who seem to think
that the discovery and utilization of opportunities to rebuke or ridicule political opponents
constitute the whole of statesmanship. However urgent the business in hand, and however
imperatively the public interests demand the
dispassionate consideration of it, the self-con-
stituted sentinel of a party discovers or invents
an opening; a partisan debate is crazily pre-
cipitated and crazily continued, and the day is
wasted. Instead of an advance toward a wise
conclusion, we have a cloud of dust which
must be cleared away before the business can be
resumed intelligently; and we are fortunate
if the resentments awakened do not tend very
strongly to unfit our legislators for the duty of
the hour.

But these spontaneous ebullitions of partisan servility are, by no means, the most pernicious manifestations of the vice which come
to the knowledge of those who observe Congressional proceedings. The case is much worse
when the welfare of the country is forgotten in
laboriously planned expedients for the acquisition of partisan advantage. Instances are not
rare in which measures of doubtful constitu-

tionality, and obviously opposed to the interests of a vast majority of the people, are de-
vised and advocated with a single eye to the
strengthening of a party through the suffrages of
a particular class of voters. Vote-catching support and vote-catching opposition engross much
of the time and intellectual strength which
ought to be devoted assiduously to the service
of unbiased and considerate patriotism. A
hostile legislative chamber, week after week, ig-
nores the most pressing public needs while ma-
nœuvring to place an administration in a false
light. For partisan advantage, men, who have
achieved high reputations for practical wisdom, surrender their own convictions and consent to be slaves of a caucus, thus robbing their
country of the personal service pledged to her
in their oaths of office. An attempt to estimate
the intellectual force diverted, in the high places
of public trust, from the service of the people
to the service of party, can result only in the
conclusion that the aggregate of such force is
incalculable.

But the evil to the country from these exhibitions of partisan servility in high places is far
from being merely negative. Even if no per-

nicious measures are put in force, the public welfare suffers great injury from such proceedings. The partisan Press is made more violent in its tone, more sophistical in its argumentation, and more untruthful in its statements. As a consequence, we witness the increasing prevalence and virulence of passions which operate, always and everywhere, against the requirements of thoughtful patriotism.

It is unnecessary to dwell on the case of those voters over whom this vice has gained but a limited control, and in whom a sense of duty to their country is sure to assert itself whenever a powerful corrective light is thrown upon the issues of the day. There is much gratification in being able to say that the number of such American citizens is already very large and is increasing rapidly from day to day. But where we are conscious of a perverse tendency, though its present force may be slight, it is well for us to hold in view the condition toward which it is impelling us.

The persons in whom partisan servility has reached an incurable stage, may be divided into two classes. Those of the first class have completely dissevered political activity from the formation ; that multitudes of old members are passing from the stage, and multitudes of new members are making their appearance every year; that the inspiring, guiding, and formative influence of one class of leaders is succeeded in a short time by that of very different leaders; that, year by year, old issues are passing into history and new issues of great moment are emerging ; that zeal for righteousness may pervade a party for a period, and then expire because its special ends are accomplished; that men of vast ability are always working energetically and untiringly to cajole or force the party with which they have connected themselves into subserviency to their own selfish aims; that the course of events is often working out, at the same time, the elevation of one party, and the deterioration of another,—that, in short, for many reasons of overwhelming weight, it may be best for the country that the same party should be triumphant at one time and be defeated at another.

We usually find the victims of partisan servility evincing a sentimentalism over which we might be mirthful, if we could shut from our view the public evils which result from it. To original assumption of their present attitudes to profound convictions. Others still are unable to give an intelligible account of the influences to which their partisan predilections and re- pugnances are due. But, in one way or an- other, it has come about that the name of their own party never fails to bring up a conception of all that is best for their country, while the name of the party to which they are opposed is suggestive of a combination of forces which threaten their country with measureless calami- ties. And these things are among the matters which they regard as having been settled for all time by considerations which admit of no question. Reasoning on the respective merits of the opposing parties, seems to them as idle as reasoning on the reality of their existence. To them a political party is an immutable entity, and the name of such a party is bound up with an unchangeable conception. In re- nouncing the high privilege of independent thought, and voluntarily descending to a state of servility, they have made themselves incapa- ble of seeing that they were not omniscient when their positions were assumed; that poli- tical parties are incessantly undergoing trans-

recognition of moral obligation. Their enslavement to their party has taken the form of chronic
hostility to the opposite party; and they have
resolved that, at all times and under all circumstances, they will fight the object of their hatred
with all the resources at their command. As
far as their influence on public affairs is concerned, they have reached that stage of personal
degradation at which " I don't care " is the spontaneous reply to a conviction of wrong-doing.
Of course they adopt the maxim, " Everything
is fair in politics ;" and the instrumentalities they
employ are chosen with exclusive reference to
their probable effectiveness, and without the
slightest regard to their moral quality.

Many of the incorrigible servile partisans of
the other class believe themselves to be loyal to
the moral government. The special enslavement in their case may be said to extend only to
their understandings, although there is obvious
guilt in the feebleness of their *desire* to understand what their country requires of them.
Some of them have inherited their political
affiliations. Others remember a time when
momentous events made their minds intensely
active, and are able with truth to ascribe the

their apprehension, the tie of political fellowship is very sweet and precious. It is fruitful
of endearment even when it binds them to
knaves and dunces. Of course, they desire to
see all the official positions in the land occupied
by members of their own party; and it dis-
tresses them exceedingly when they find a political opponent acting as a constable, a cross-
roads postmaster, or a book-keeper or porter in
a public office. They seem to believe that there
is something in the political appellation assumed by themselves and those in fellowship
with them, which, in some mysterious way, gives
to those who bear it a special fitness for serving writs, stamping letters, copying documents
and handling boxes. On the other hand, it has
become impossible for them to admit that the
most capable and upright of their political opponents can withstand the disqualifying force
of the name which designates their partisan relations. Fitness for the public service, in their
view, is the product of devotion to their party;
and natural capacity, experience, and proved
fidelity have no connection with it. Hence,
when a high official belonging to their party
leaves undisturbed a political opponent whom

he has power to remove, he is guilty of a crime but little short of treason. It is probable that we find, at this point, the highest manifestation of the fruitfulness of sentimentalism in the begetting of silliness.

Servile partisans are very apt to be proud of their servility. There is often an unctuous boastfulness in their tones when they say: " I'm a Democrat," or " I'm a Republican," as the case may be ; and " I go with my party all the time. You won't find *me* kicking or scratching. The candidates of my party are *my* candidates, and wherever my party goes, I'll follow it." When one of this class is made frank by grogginess, he may be heard to say : " If my party nominates the *devil, I'll* support him." But exultant avowals of determined slavishness are not confined to the circles of the ignorant. On occasions, even the halls of Congress are made to resound with them, and there are grotesque assumptions of superiority to the statesmen who choose to maintain their self-respect by the application of common-sense to matters which concern the public service. A flood of sparkling ridicule, bubbling with contemptuous similes, is poured out upon the men

who prefer freedom to slavery ; and eminent
Senators roll in their chairs, completely un-
manned by approving mirth.   Such exhibitions
enable us to observe how easy it is for a man
to mistake in himself the strength of a blind
passion for strength of understanding, and thus
to arrive at a very absurd estimate of the value
of his own personality.

The immediate effects of partisan servility,
in determining the results of political contests,
are not its most pernicious fruits.   In contemplating the perilous experiment of universal
suffrage, we have a source of great comfort in
the fact that the servile partisans, as well as the
corruptible voters and the citizens utterly incapable of voting intelligently, are divided between the parties.   In so far as this division
approximates equality, the power of these
classes over immediate results is nullified.   We
see most clearly the enormous mischievousness
of the vice now under consideration, when we
think of it as an instrumentality controlled
by unscrupulous demagogues.   The question,
" Which party shall rule ?" is far less important
to the country than the question, "By whom
shall the parties, respectively, be molded and

led?" In proportion as the leadership of a party is characterized by earnest patriotism, personal integrity and practical wisdom, its policy will answer the demands of public welfare, while, as a rule, its measures and aims will be inimical to the interests of the people in proportion as it shall fall under the sway of the incompetent and selfish. This is the ever-present status, whatever the respective traditions of the parties may be.

Now, it is notorious that tricky politicians are always struggling for leadership, while patriotic men, who cannot be induced to forfeit their self-respect, restrict themselves to *earning* a title to political influence by the unselfish improvement of such opportunities as may present themselves. With the former class, leadership is the paramount object of endeavor; but with the latter class it is made to wait on meritorious service. The demagogues, therefore, start out with the advantage which always accrues from keeping a single point steadily in view and bending all energies to its accomplishment. It is unhappily true, also, that a selfish motive has an energizing force which, in ordinary times, we cannot expect to find in pat-

riotic impulses. All the considerations which
bear upon their personal fortunes are stimulating the professional politicians to struggle for
dominant influence in their respective parties,
while the like incentives to exertion have little
to do with the unselfish efforts by which such
influence is merited. Nevertheless, the demagogue's selfishness would be self-defeating in
every instance, if all partisans were *free* partisans and independently thoughtful concerning their political duties. The two classes of
men would then be seen to be what they are;
the intriguers would be repudiated, and self-for-
getful patriotism united with capability would
be rewarded with dominant influence.

But partisan servility is wholly incompatible
with independent thought on public affairs.
For the servile partisan the conventions of his
party have all the authority of an infallible
church; and his blind trust yields him a sufficient reason for indulging his tendency to intellectual laziness. The cunning manipulator
of conventions understands that the candidates
whom he causes to be put forward are sure of
support, and that no difficulty in electing them
will arise from the fact that they are base

enough to be subservient to his personal designs. Moreover, he finds, in pandering to the prejudices and passions of servile partisans, such a resource for extending his power as self-respecting patriots scorn to employ. His hearers exult and feel themselves to be personally commended as he sets forth, with the wildest extravagance, the claims of their party; and the more atrocious the falsehoods which he mingles with his denunciations of the opposite party, the more loudly they shout: "HE is the man to lead us to victory." They see in him "the consummate flower ' of the vice by which they are enslaved, and, consequently, treat him as a representative of the highest virtue. His intrigues and "deals" for self-aggrandizement are justified as illustrations of devotion to a party on whose success all human welfare hangs; and overwhelming evidence of his corruptness is repelled without examination. When we consider that men of this class, unscrupulous in their methods and skillful in playing on the weaknesses of their fellow-partisans, are working untiringly in all parts of the land, we get a partial view of the magnitude of the danger that all parties will be demoralized and made unpa-

triotic through the successful employment of
partisan servility as an instrumentality for the
acquisition of political control.

If we had not all learned by experience that
our predilections and aversions are always tend-
ing insidiously and potently to warp our judgments and move us to act unreasonably, the
host of intelligent men, who honestly intend to
be patriotic citizens and still are to be found in
the ranks of servile partisans, would awaken our
astonishment. To know that cunning demagogues are utilizing his weaknesses for their own
advancement, cannot be agreeable to any man.
Nobody likes to think of himself as a tool.
And yet that great body of American voters,
who follow the leaders of their respective parties blindly, and can be counted on for the in-
variable support of regular nominees, are in
constant danger of being reduced to that pitch
of degradation. By as much as a voter's actions
evince a determination to adhere to his party
under all circumstances, by so much he does
violence to his personal dignity. Partisan servility cannot be made compatible with thorough
manliness.

It is equally obvious that every concession

to this vice is a derogation from the claims of patriotism. " What is best for my country?" is the only question which a voter has a right to treat as paramount, when he is about to take action upon matters which concern the welfare of his country; and if he lays it down as an un-changeable rule, that the public interests are necessarily and always bound up with the suc-cess of his party, he is no longer to be credited with the patriotic exercise of common-sense. In so far as an American voter, capable of fore-thinking the consequences of proposed meas-ures and of estimating the qualifications of can-didates, shall decline to make a re-survey of the field, before deciding upon the line of action he shall adopt in a political contest that is drawing near, to that extent he is lacking in genuine patriotism.

In connection with the perversions of all our structurally necessitated impulses, there is need of careful discrimination. It is often exceed-ingly difficult to fix upon the point where vir-tue ends and vice begins; and skill in such discriminations is to be numbered among the highest fruits of self-culture. We encounter this difficulty in the case before us. It is not

easy to draw the line between free partisanship and partisan servility, not easy to lay down
a rule or a set of rules, according to which men
are to be classed as " free partisans," or as " servile partisans." Nevertheless, those who aspire
to be of the former class will usually find befitting diligence rewarded with a clear view of the
path of duty. My own reflections have conducted me to the acceptance of the following
propositions :

1. _There is a presumption in favor of the con-
tinuance of existing affiliations._

Without a certain measure of stability there
can be no weight of character. A change of
position, in the absence of conviction, denotes
a capriciousness quite as far from the line of
duty on the one side as an unreasoning obsti-
nacy is on the other. Moreover, as a rule, our
highest efficiency can be realized for a time
in the organization with which we have been accustomed to work. Such channels of influence
are open to us there as we cannot hope to utilize
at once in the opposing organization. It is
right, therefore, for us to hold that the burden
of proof is upon those who would influence us
to change our partisan relations.

2. *Partisanship coincides with patriotism at all points when it moves us to work for the elevation of our respective parties.*

I have often thought this to be the most important field of patriotic endeavor for those of us who are not called upon to deal officially with affairs of state. Every affection, going out to human beings, discloses its highest mission when it operates for the raising of its objects to a higher plane. Indeed, the desire which is called "self-love" makes its divine origin most clear when it inspires us to struggle upward in the scale of being. The personal worthiness of their children is a possession in comparison with which all else, that parents can crave for them, is wholly insignificant. Unquestionably, the citizen is rendering to his community the highest service of which he is capable, when he is aiding the prevalence of intelligence and virtue. It is clear, finally, that the highest end of American patriotism is the worthiness of the American people. The future history of our country—her experiences of weal and of woe,—must depend chiefly on the characteristics to be displayed by our fellow-countrymen in the years before us. Inevitably, those characteristics will be reflected in the workings of our institutions. The average intellectual and moral worth of our people will be represented in the making and execution of our laws ; and there will be no suspension of the immutable decree, that wisdom and righteousness shall be fruitful of good, while ignorance and iniquity shall be productive only of evil. It is for the free partisan to keep these things in view, and to feel that his own party presents a special field for the exercise of his patriotism in this highest form. Then his partisanship will immensely re-enforce his patriotism, and greatly enhance the public value of his personality. In so far as he aids in elevating worthy men to the leadership of his party, and promotes the adjustment of its aims to the principles of rectitude, he will deserve well of his country.

We ought never to lose sight of the *reflex* operation of political activity. We cannot enter heartily into the support of men and measures without having our own characters receive an impress in return. We cannot contend for the elevation of a man whose integrity is questionable, without a diminution of our own regard for integrity. If we assent to a measure of doubtful rectitude, because our party has committed itself to it, we are sure to suffer a relaxation of our moral principles. As it is with us in these respects, so is it with all our fellow-citizens. The demoralizing influences which may flow back upon the great body of a party, from dishonesty in its leaders and un-righteousness in its measures, are absolutely incalculable ; and the demoralization having once begun, it is likely to go forward at a con-stantly accelerated pace. At each stage of moral decay a party is prepared to sustain still baser leaders, more unjustifiable methods and more unrighteous measures. Thus arises the danger, that the action and reaction be-tween the body of a party and its controllers will be increasingly pernicious. On the other hand, zealous exertion, in support of upright leaders and of measures which commend themselves to the moral sense of the people, cannot fail to elevate the tone of a party and to make it in all ways more patriotic. At this point we obtain a glimpse of the inesti-mable services rendered their country, by the men who devote themselves ably and ear-

nestly to the purification of their respective
parties.

3. *Partisanship is perverted whenever it is
allowed to determine the results of elections purely
local.*

Every special affection has its legitimate
sphere, and becomes an evil agent so far as it
transcends the limits prescribed for it in the
creative design.   It then robs other affections
of the force which they ought to have as factors
in personal life.   That is precisely the way in
which all worthy affections are liable to be
turned into vicious passions.   It is thus that a
misguided love of kindred, for example, sometimes engrosses the powers of men to such an
extent, that they are indifferent to the welfare
of the community in which they live, careless
of the interests of their country, and even for-
getful of moral obligation.   The perversion is
quite as manifest when a man permits the love
of party to engross the power and command the
efforts which should be placed at the service of
a desire to protect and advance the interests of
his community.

Whatever the matter to be determined, the
bringing in of considerations which have no re-

lation to it cannot be otherwise than harmful ; and when such considerations become paramount, the consequences are apt to be disastrous. But the issues on which national parties divide can have no possible connection with affairs which lie under the exclusive control of local authorities. So far, then, as attention is drawn away to those issues when provision is to be made for interests purely local, the popular mind is unfitted for the work in hand. This is not the worst. Partisan servility is introduced, with all its power to distort the intellectual vision of voters. Thus comes an aggravation of their unfitness to judge of the comparative merits of candidates, and of the expediency or inexpediency of what is proposed in regard to the local matters which call for action.

It is because of this perversion of partisanship that municipal governments often fall under the sway of professional politicians who care for nothing beyond the advancement of their personal fortunes. A cunning and unscrupulous member of the dominant party is elevated to leadership in each ward or district ; and those leaders constitute the actual government of the city. Subserviency to them is the indispensable condition of political success, and efficiency in the management of voters comes to be treated as the supreme qualification for office. Growing numbers of men perceive that their votes have a cash value; unofficial agents demand a high price for their services ; some of the officials find their vices enormously expensive, while others of them are in haste to be rich, and, all this time, contractors are offering large rewards for the privilege of thrusting their hands into the public treasury. Day by day, the corruption grows more pervasive, and its pressure increases, till the covering which has been held over it gives way, and we have an explosion which arrests the attention of the country for a brief period. Then the politicians quietly begin their preparations for another long campaign against the public. All these things are done in the name of party ; and none of them could take place in the absence of partisan servility.

I know that many honest men excuse the carrying of national politics into local elections on the ground that this is essential to the maintenance of their party's organization. This view is based on the assumption that the destiny of a party is under the absolute control of professional politicians, to whom the mass of voters yield unquestioning obedience. Is it a just conception of government by the people that is thus evinced? If we were compelled to say, " It is true that our government is carried on through parties thus controlled and obedience thus rendered," it would then be our duty to ask: " *Ought* it to be true ?—Shall it continue to be true?" I aver that any man, who is fit to be entrusted with the ballot, can sustain his party with all heartiness at a national or state election, and dismiss political issues from his mind when he is dealing with matters to which they have no legitimate relation. There is no more necessity of political bias at an election of local officials than there is at an election of railroad directors, and no better justification of it in the one case than in the other.

The fundamental error in this matter is the impression that a party can be strengthened by meddling with purely local affairs. Every organization suffers a diminution of actual strength when it goes beyond its appropriate

sphere. Our recent political history is fruitful
of lessons which free partisans should take to
heart. Look at the almost inextinguishable
odium which parties have incurred through ex-
posures of criminal officials elevated to places
of municipal trust as representatives and
champions of those parties. Consider, too,
how strenuously and persistently powerful
bodies of local leaders have endeavored to extend their demoralizing sway over the state and
national councils of their respective parties.
Finally, does not every well-informed person
know that those local partisan leaders, who are
bound together by the tie of common selfishness, are always ready to *betray* their party ?
Free partisanship unites with patriotism in
summoning us to resolve that, so far as we are
concerned, political affiliations shall have no influence on the results of local elections. If all
intelligent and unselfish voters would take this
position, no great harm would result from partisan nominations ; for no party would then
dare to present candidates by whose official action the public interests would be endangered.

4. *The support of an untrustworthy man for
a position of public trust is always unpatriotic.*

No man can justify to himself the treatment of public interests according to a rule which he would not apply in the management of his private interests. Indeed, a thoroughly honorable man, when he is neither blinded by prejudice, nor unduly hurried by passion, is always made more considerate and careful by the reflection, that his actions will affect the welfare of others, no less than his own. When he can say " Nobody else will be hurt," it is possible for him to feel at liberty to obey his inclinations somewhat heedlessly. But in proportion as he clearly apprehends that his proceedings must have important consequences for others, he becomes conscious of moral responsibility, and the sense of duty asserts its rightful supremacy in the control of his conduct. Of course, his desire to do what ought to be done is greatly strengthened when he perceives that the consequences in view concern an object of his warm affection. If he loves his country, therefore, his conscience will be supported by his patriotism in forbidding the negligent treatment of public interests. But is any man ready to commit his private affairs to the charge of a person whose integrity he distrusts?

Would any man advise a friend to do such a thing?

No one can point out a limit to the evil which may result from the elevation of a dishonest man to an important official position. But a small part of it is found in the immediate consequences of his official misconduct. He holds out to aspiring young men what seems to them a demonstration of popular indifference to uprightness in character ; and baneful influences are constantly flowing from his success to the myriads who recognize no higher standard than public opinion. New channels are opened for the demoralizing energy by which his elevation has been achieved ; and all the elements of mastery in his nature are serving to undermine the principles of other officials,—to corrupt them and make them corrupters in their turn. Who can tell within what limits the hellish processes will be confined ?

It is not probable that we shall ever have the privilege of supporting a candidate in whom we can see no faults. It is certain that no such opportunity will present itself. But there is no lack of competent men who can be relied upon to aim at thorough fidelity in discharging such trusts as may be committed to them ; and patriotic partisans cannot be too prompt in demonstrating that such men, and such men alone, can be clothed with official responsibility. Genuine patriotism requires us to set it down as an inviolable rule, that no ballot of ours is ever to be cast for a man of questionable integrity.

5. *A party may often be strengthened by the defeat of one or more of its nominees.*

Such an event, resulting from the unworthiness of the defeated candidate, proves the presence in the party of a strong regulative force whose end is the public welfare. To that extent the party is commended to the favor of intelligent voters. Moreover, free partisans are thus incited to a more vigilant guardianship of their party's credit ; and a salutary lesson is taught the men who are disposed to activity in connection with nominating conventions. Unless demoralization has already gone far enough to demand an overwhelming defeat, the net result is an obvious strengthening of the party's title to popular support, and an improvement in its prospects.

6. *An unqualified determination, to adhere*

under all circumstances to any party composed of human beings, is never justifiable.

I suppose that this determination is avowed by scarcely any person who is likely to glance at these pages, though very frequent expressions of it, in one form or another, may be heard by one who listens to the more ignorant voters. It is true, too, that, in studying the mental states of many highly intelligent men, we see reasons for classing a change in their partisan affiliations among impossible events. I have already accounted sufficiently for such a state of mind, and we are called upon here to consider only how far a self-respecting man can justify it to himself.

There are many relations which it is reasonable to treat as established for all time. The right attitude toward the moral government, toward mankind and toward one's country should be an unchangeable attitude. But the justifiableness of a subsidiary relation must always depend on the requirements of the higher relation. This is the case before us. The true end of a political party is the welfare of a country; and that is the only ground on which partisan affiliation can be vindicated. Now, is any man prepared to set it down, as beyond debate, that the dominancy of his party will be best for his country through all time? No man can foresee what the composition of his party will be, or what the ruling elements within it will be, a few years hence. No man can predict the altered circumstances which will call for new features of policy, or foretell the respective positions of parties in regard to the now unthought-of measures which will be demanded by the public interests. The truth is, that nothing less than prophetic vision could justify a man in resolving upon his relations to parties for any considerable period in the future.

7. *A party forfeits its title to continued adhesion in so far as it submits to the sway of unprincipled men.*

In its relations to the public welfare, a party's character is determined by the influences which are dominant among its leaders. Its traditions have nothing to do with the beneficence or injuriousness of its present aims and tendencies; and no conclusion upon such matters can be reached through an estimate of the average worthiness of its members. A few men give shape to the policy of a party, and assume the responsibility of committing five millions of voters to the support of it. A few men determine what aims a party's success shall make paramount in national legislation, and what spirit it shall cause to flow from the head of the government and pervade the civil service of the country. In short, at any given period, a party is patriotic or unpatriotic, according as its most influential leaders are the one or the other.

We often find it difficult to compare the parties with each other in this respect. Influential leaders are apt to be, at the same time, objects of high encomium, and of vehement detraction. If we make all due allowance for extravagance of language, and diligently seek the real truth, we shall see that good influences and bad influences are at work on each side. Still, there are always some indices which may afford us much help. We may turn our attention, for example, upon the able leaders who have earned an unquestionable reputation for probity and freedom from misleading passions, and ask to what extent they are deferred to by their fellow-partisans. We may ascertain what weight, on each side, is at-

tached to the wishes and utterances of conspicuous demagogues. We may compare the
leaders of the respective parties as to the
habit of diverting time and thought from the
public business to the manufacture of personal
or political "capital." We may consider the
breadth of patriotism evinced, respectively, by
the two classes of leaders—the extent to which
they respectively regard the welfare of all sec-
tions of their country. We may watch for
manifestations, on each side, of a tendency to
subordinate general interests to special interests. We may see how far each class of leaders is ready to pander to the prejudices and
passions of the ignorant and vicious. Finally,
it behooves us to study the proceedings of national conventions, and to satisfy ourselves
thoroughly as to the grades of morality represented in their nominations and in the treatment which they bestow upon the questions
of the day.

8. *The rise of a party to superiority in patri-*
otic aims makes the transfer of support to it an
obvious duty.

No one will dispute this proposition. All
partisans claim such superiority for their re-

spective parties, and defend their positions on that ground. It is true that we sometimes hear base appeals to the selfishness of a particular class of voters; but to the credit of human nature, we may say that, as a rule, the partisan orator, who cares for nothing beyond his own advancement, finds it expedient to maintain that the supremacy of his party is indispensable to the welfare of his country. It is an *intellectual* duty that is s t before us at this point; and each voter must determine for himself with what degree of intellectual liberty he shall survey the political field and institute comparisons between the parties. As we are all prone to the vices which I have discussed, and all quite sure to come short of our own ideals, it becomes us to aim at absolute freedom from bias. Nothing less than this can satisfy the demands of thoroughgoing patriotism.

Minds are constituted so differently, and there are so many points to be considered, that we shall not all reach the same conclusion. But if we are honest with ourselves, we shall be apt to see our several ways clear; and it will then be right for each one of us,

either in the old relation or in a new relation,
to have his efficiency increased by the energizing force of party spirit.

It is proper for us now to investigate some
of the

DUTIES INCIDENT TO FREE PARTISANSHIP.

I have already spoken of the most important of these,—the duty, namely, of laboring
for the elevation of one's party.   I have shown
that all efforts thus directed are in perfect
accord with the requirements of patriotism.
This is one of those truths which are too plain
for argument, and yet fail of general apprehension.   The number of intelligent voters, who
evince no sense of responsibility for the characters of their respective parties, is immense.
It is hardly too much to say, that, in general,
the men who are best fitted to give tone and
direction to a party, are the men who are
accustomed to neglect that service.   In any
given year, their political activity is restricted
to the period which follows the declaration of
principles and the placing of candidates in the
field ; and it is often restricted to the day of
election.   What moral sentiments, and what

measure of practical wisdom shall be reflected in the battle-cries, and represented in the characters of candidates, and what shall be the reflex influence of partisan effort, are matters with which they do not concern themselves.

It is easy enough to account for this general abstention from the work preliminary to political contests. The pursuits, studies and tastes of many partisans are unfavorable to familiarity with public affairs. By reason of this fact, they have come to take it for granted that their party embodies such wisdom and patriotism as will secure it from misguidance, and from the dominancy of evil influences. Apprehending no danger to their party from such sources, they feel no sense of duty pressing them to exertion for which they have no taste. They think of the preliminary work only in its bearing on the prospect of success at the ballot-box, and excuse their inactivity on the ground that the necessary measures are sure to be taken by men who have ample experience in such matters. The radical error in these cases is the entertainment of a degree of confidence which ought never to be reposed in a political party. Facts, which ought to be fresh in the minds of all American citizens, are sufficient to convince any candid person that such parties are always liable to the rapid decay of all that is best in them, and to the rapid growth within them of enormous abuses. I have already pointed out the sources of this danger, and shown that it is imminent at all times. But, if we could be justified in regarding our parties as secure from deterioration, that assurance ought not to satisfy us. Is there a patriotic partisan in the land who does not feel that his party ought to occupy a higher plane? Does any such man see all the wisdom and unselfishness that he desires to see in the leaders of his party? Can we be satisfied when we compare the exhibitions of unadulterated zeal for the public welfare with the efforts put forth for partisan advantage? The more we reflect on this subject the more deeply we shall feel that the elevation of all parties is needful to our country ; and I see no way in which a thoughtful partisan can free himself from responsibility in the matter.

If we analyze our disinclination to preliminary partisan work, and compare what is usually done in that line with what ought to be done, our dissatisfaction with ourselves will increase. We shall see what we have regarded as a consciousness of unfitness for such service, resolving itself into a love of ease—into laziness. However modest a view we may take of our own abilities, none of us are deterred from endeavoring to influence our fellow-men when we have a powerful motive impelling us to do so. Our trouble lies in the feebleness with which our partisanship subserves our patriotism. To be sure, our disinclination is strengthened by repugnance to association with such men as we often see to be most active in marshalling parties for impending contests. We are aware, also, that, without self-degradation, we cannot engage in such intrigues as we see to be common with professional politicians. But when our hearts are thoroughly stirred in behalf of an enterprise, we never allow ourselves to be kept aloof from it by considerations pertaining to the characters of those with whom we may be brought in contact. Besides, if patriotic partisans should become active in this preliminary work, they would be apt to find themselves contending earnestly against the trading politicians, instead of being intimately associated with them. Far from degrading themselves by complicity in the practices of the unworthy, they would be going up higher by manfully struggling for the defeat of corrupt combinations and for the introduction of commendable methods.

The truth is that, in almost every locality in the land, each party presents within itself a battle-ground from which free partisans cannot stay away without derogation from their loyalty. I make no reference here to such warring factions as we see in every populous community. Their struggles, for the most part, are contests over opportunities to live and prosper at the public expense; and such warfare is usually made more furious and more regardless of moral decency by the ambitions of rival leaders. The battle to which free partisans are called is of a very different kind. The work immediately before them is the demonstration that their party cannot be used as a tool of personal selfishness, and that success within it is no longer to be achieved by immoral combinations and practices. They are to deliver their party from servility to the unprincipled, and restore it to the ministration of patriotism. It is true that this result presupposes a great change in the impressions and actions of some millions of our most enlightened citizens. We need, at the outset, a reformation, if not a revolution, in public opinion. There are large circles in which it is deemed scarcely respectable to participate in caucuses and nominating conventions. Many of us find it hard to utter the word "politician," without curling our lips contemptuously; and political activity is quite commonly regarded as an indication of moral degeneracy.

Now, what do these things prove? Simply this: That the great body of free partisans, who have no ends of their own to serve in connection with public affairs, are accustomed to let their respective parties become as "clay in the hands of the potter," to men who are stimulated to political activity by that selfishness which is always manifesting its power in disgraceful methods. The simple fact, that partisan activity is widely suggestive of personal baseness, is overwhelming proof of a general dereliction of duty. If the true end of a party is the welfare of a country, why should not every patriotic citizen be active in strengthen-

ing his party by keeping it adjusted to that end?
It is unquestionable that the overshadowing
need of the United States to-day, is the recognition, by the great body of intelligent voters,
of their responsibility for the characters of their
respective parties. The most ominous circumstance, connected with our national prospects,
is the fact that the characters of political parties, to an alarming extent, are shaped by their
unworthiest members. But can any man fail
to see that the formative power resides in those
preliminary measures of which I am speaking?
Before the great majority of those best qualified for patriotic work have put forth an effort,
the parties have already become what they
must continue to be till the end of the contest.
The issues are joined, the battle-cries are chos-
en, the candidates are in the field, and nothing
remains but the simple struggle for victory.
How far the triumph of this party or of that
would benefit or injure the country, has already been determined ; and an immense majority of the best American citizens have con-
tributed nothing at all toward the solution of
the momentous problem.

The pessimistic view, that selfishness and

ignorance must continue to be dominant in determining the levels at which political parties
shall stand, is wholly unworthy of those who
believe in government by the people. Throughout the land, the voters who aim only at what
they deem the public good, constitute an overwhelming majority in each party. Such voters have power to preclude all base leadership,
and utterly to crush all partisan bands of plun-
derers. They can secure to the people the
services of their wisest fellow-countrymen, and
make salutary influences paramount in regu-
lating the aims of their respective parties. The
one prerequisite to these results is the befitting
education of public opinion. For this we must
rely largely on the partisan press. Let partisan
journalists apprehend that their highest public
duty concerns the characters of their parties,
and that making a party *worthy* of success is
the highest partisan service within the limits of
human power. Let them understand, and
cause their readers to understand, that this
end cannot be realized without the vigilance
and activity of the great body of enlightened
voters. Let them be " instant in season, out
of season," giving " line upon line; precept

upon precept." Then we may hope for the
early dawning of an era wherein strife between
parties shall resolve itself into patriotic emula-
tion.

The habit of participating in preliminary
partisan work should be formed and maintained,
although conditions differ with times and lo-
calities, and there may be occasions in which
the voter will see no especial need of his inter-
position. It may seem to him that all those
who are seeking nominations are equally unob-
jectionable. I am inclined to express myself
on a matter of taste which comes in at this
point. The maxim, that "The office should
seek the man, and not the man the office," is
often repeated with approval; but I am convinced that it ought to be discarded. The co-
operation of our desire for personal welfare,
with the impulses which move us to work
for the public good, is obviously provided for
in our spiritual constitution. If perversion
were always absent, and comprehensive wisdom
were always present, pure benevolence would
be constantly re-enforced by desire of happiness. It is well, therefore, that patriotic impulses are made more effective by personal

aspirations; and we have only to see to it that our rule of action be prescribed by the superior motives, and that we avoid the enormous blunder of making our personal aims paramount. If a man is conscious of disposition and ability to serve the public efficiently, I see no reason why he should not seek opportunities to render such service. Nominations are sure to be sought, and we are under obligations to men of high character when they contest for them successfully over men of low character. It is unquestionable that the public has often suffered great loss through the distastefulness of such contests to able and upright men; and it seems to me that there would be great public gain in the universal suppression of the sentiment embodied in the maxim which I have quoted.

If we are diligent in observing the men who seek nominations, we shall seldom fail to discover some grounds of choice among them. They are quite sure to display their leading characteristics in the methods they adopt, and in the arguments they employ. The cunning and the true-hearted, the competent and the incompetent, alike, will reveal themselves.

We shall see how far the advancement of one or another of them would contribute to the strengthening or weakening of a " ring," that is aiming to make tools of us, and shall be able to select the man who can be counted on most confidently to hold himself aloof from unwor thy intrigues. In these and many other ways our constant vigilance and readiness for activity will help our party to deserve success at the ballot-box.

Even when free partisans are fully determined to keep the public interests in view at primary meetings and nominating conventions, they are still exceedingly liable to be misled. For my own part, I have often found it necessary to be on my guard against my personal predilections. The fact, that a man's society is agreeable to me, comes far short of proving that he is qualified for an official position to which he may be aspiring. There is a certain geniality of disposition, combined with fluency of entertaining utterance, which is often found quite apart from the essential elements of efficiency, and never affords proof of the moral solidity indispensable to trustworthiness. On the other hand we sometimes find, among those who are least companionable, men whose judgments are seldom in fault, and who can be trusted without reserve in whatever positions they may be placed. There is no constant relation between the qualities which make social intercourse agreeable, and those which constitute fitness for the public service, though, of course, there is no incompatibility between the two sets of characteristics. Through lack of discrimination, there is apt to be an undue advantage on the side of one who can make an entertaining or exciting speech. It is taken for granted that he is a man of ability, and will show himself to be such in any sphere to which he may aspire. Whether the office in question calls for oratorical power or presents no occasion for it, is a matter that is not considered. Moreover, no reflection is bestowed on the difference between the declamation which may be effective on the "stump" and the public speaking which is convincing in a deliberative assembly. It is plain that careful and discriminating thought is prerequisite to a judicious choice between aspirants for nomination. Each case is to be studied by itself, and studied with exclusive reference to qualifications for a particular position. A little foresight will enable the free partisan to see that, besides being the only patriotic course, this is the most expedient course for his party. Whatever may be the immediate results, a party is sure in the end to suffer loss of credit and loss of strength whenever it subordinates fitness for office to what is called "availability." As a rule, too, that short-sighted measure disappoints those who count on its efficacy for even temporary success. When you cannot boldly and honestly challenge a comparison between the qualifications of your candidate and those of his competitor, you are but poorly equipped for an appeal to voters. Evasion of that question is always treated as a suspicious circumstance; and apologies are wretched material in electioneering.

I believe in systematic partisan work, in regular nominations and in properly regulated "discipline." In the political history of every free country, occasions arrive when many sagacious and patriotic men find themselves detached from all parties, and constitute what, in imitation of the French, we may call "The Centre." They have no expectation of controlling the government themselves, but are watchful to preclude the possession of its high places by unworthy politicians; and their service is often of incalculable value to the people. Most of us, however, always see our way clear to identification with one or the other of the great parties; and it becomes us to consider diligently what is befitting that relation. I am satisfied that the "machinery" of caucusses and conventions, though fearfully abused at times, is, on the whole, beneficent. I think that aspirations to elective positions should manifest themselves first through those preliminary assemblages, and that announcements of candidacy, irrespective of regular nominations, should be discountenanced. My views concerning the true limitations of party fealty have been set forth in the propositions discussed on former pages. The sum of the matter is this: Before each political contest, we are to labor most earnestly to furnish our respective parties with such candidates, and so to direct their aims, that they shall deserve to be triumphant; and upon our success, or failure, in these endeavors, our subsequent actions are to depend.

Passing from the discussion of duties pertaining to elective offices, let us now consider the voter's

Responsibility for the Character of the Civil Service.

Considerably more than a hundred thousand of what are called "Federal offices" are filled by executive appointment. The Governors of the several States have an appointing power of greater or less extent; and the municipal service of the country is largely provided for in the same way. Hence, a very large part of the public business is transacted by officials in the choice of whom no direct action can be taken at the ballot box. Nevertheless, it will occur to every one that voters in general have a weighty responsibility in the matter. It is for them to determine by whom that appointing power shall be wielded ; and it is scarcely possible to exaggerate the importance to the public welfare of such decisions. When a man solicits our support for a position to which many places of trust are subordinate, our duty requires us to investigate very carefully his qualifications for that selection of pub-

lic servants which we are desired to delegate
to him. He may be wholly unqualified for the
bestowal of offices, while capable of high efficiency in other spheres. The question of paramount importance concerns the end which he
may be expected to keep in view. Do his
characteristics afford assurance of an honest
and steadfast regard to the public interests?
Will he simply aim to have the people faith-
fully and efficiently served? Have we reason
to apprehend that he will employ patronage as
an instrument of sordid ambition? Is he a
servile partisan? Do his partisan predilections
and animosities make him incapable of a fair
estimate of qualifications? Will he require his
subordinates to divert to the service of party
the time and attention for which they are paid
from the public treasury? These are some of
the questions which ought to be entertained
whenever the appointing power is to be vested
by the popular vote. And other questions re-
main when these are disposed of satisfactorily.
An appointing officer needs to be a superior
judge of men, and to have due confidence in
that superiority. He should be capable of
justly estimating the recommendations which

may be placed before him; and his desire to please should never hurry him to a premature conclusion. The anger of rejected applicants and their patrons should have no terror for him.

But the responsibility of which I am speaking is far from being limited to matters which concern the characters of those for whom our votes are solicited. The whole question of conferring official functions by executive appointment is now before American voters, and calling for action at their hands. They are required to choose between two *systems* which are so well understood that an extended description of them here would be superfluous. Everyone is familiar with the main features of what are known, respectively, as "the spoils system" and "the merit system." The former was acquiesced in universally by the American people for nearly fifty years. The latter, having been established triumphantly in Great Britain, through a struggle which lasted a third of a century, began to be commended to us a few years ago, and a limited application of it has already enabled us to judge of its fruits. Without reference to the lines on which parties

have divided heretofore, voters are now rang-
ing themselves as to preference between these
two systems. On the one side we have a demand for re-action and the total abandonment
of the merit system ; on the other, the watch-
word is "onward," and the extension of the
merit system is earnestly advocated. This is
by far the most momentous issue ever presented to American voters in a time of peace.
It goes to the very heart of the question, "In
what spirit shall the government of the United
States be conducted ?" We are called upon to
decide whether the interests of the whole
people, or the interests of partisan leaders,
shall be made paramount in the transaction of
the public business. I think no one, who has
thought it worth while to read the foregoing
pages of this essay, can be in doubt as to my
position on this issue. All the conclusions
which I have stated are in perfect harmony
with the approval of the merit system, while
many of them are entirely irreconcilable with
a preference for the spoils system. I am in
complete sympathy with those who are laboring to make the Civil Service non-partisan so
far as that result is compatible with the effi-

ciency of our principal administrative officers. As the changes contemplated by reformers can never be reached without a prolonged · struggle, it is well for us to investigate the forces with which we must contend. To this end I present the following

Analysis of the Anti-Reform Spirit.

Of course, there is a certain variety in the mental states which can always be counted on for resistance to the correction of abuses. The different elements blend in varying proportions, one or another of them being predominant; and, in some cases, a part of them seem to be wholly wanting. Still, each of them is a force which the reformer is sure to encounter. The first element in hostility to the merit system, I find to be that

PARTISAN SENTIMENTALISM

of which I have already spoken in discussing " Partisan Servility." It indicates the usurpation by feeling of the prerogatives of reason, and often goes very far in the direction of making its victim idiotic. What kind of a jumble Sentimentalism is capable of producing among the faculties of an able man is illustrated in the following language from the pen of a distinguished United States Senator:

" I am opposed to that pretentious humbug because I am a Democrat, and, as such, I believe that Democratic principles are best administered by Democrats in office ; and, finally, I prefer my friends to my enemies, as gratitude and common decency enjoin upon all men, except, of course, Mugwump reformers.".

If the Senator had not been pressed for time he would have shown us, undoubtedly, how "Democratic principles" might prove their salutariness in the clerical work of the departments at Washington and in the transaction of business at the few post offices and custom-houses to which the Civil Service law now extends. It is to be regretted that he did not point out the beautiful manner in which opposition to a high tariff and support of the same, approval and disapproval of silver coinage and other contrarieties brought to light in Congressional divisions, combine to work out the perfection of a copyist. It is *something* to be able to perceive what exists; but this is little in comparison with the ability yielded by Sentimentalism for the discovery of nonexistent relations. Men of the unsentimental sort are unable to see how the color of an eye can affect the nail on a toe, or what political principles have to do with personal efficiency.

But the Senator prefers his " friends " to his "enemies." He would have us understand, of course, that all Democrats are his friends and all Republicans his enemies. The tie of political fellowship has lifted him above, or dragged him below, the influences which enter into the friendships and enmities of the unsentimental. Personal characteristics vanish from sight in the presence of this overshadowing relation. But we have not yet attended to all the beauties disclosed in the Senator's language. It is plainly implied that he looks upon friendship to himself as the supreme qualification for office. This may raise a question as to the expediency of committing the control of the government to him, or to any one who agrees with him. There are fifty millions of us who are as much affected as he is by the manner in which the official work of the country is performed. We have some interest in the motives which shall bear sway, and in the tests which shall be applied, when pub-

lic servants are to be selected; and I am not
prepared to concede that the friendships and
enmities of any appointing officer afford the
guidance that would be safest for us. I remember that a President-elect was once ap-
plauded throughout the land for declaring
that he had "no friends to reward nor enemies to punish" in the distribution of offices.
Unless public opinion has greatly changed, it
still condemns the forgetting of public interests in the gratification of personal predilections. I do not believe that the historical
connection of odium with "nepotism" and
"favoritism" in public life is altogether a
thing of the past, nor that abstinence from
the practices thus named is generally held to
be violative of the obligations of "gratitude
and common decency." The obvious truth is,
that an appointing officer is unfaithful to his
trust whenever he allows his attention to be
diverted from the needs of the service by his
feelings, whether they spring from a common
relation to parties, or whatever may be their
source. Indeed, a preference, founded on
a community of political affiliation, when no
political principle is involved, is less excusable

than nepotism. We can make allowance for
an error due to love of kindred, when we
should recognize no palliation of a similar
error growing out of party spirit. Plain as all
these things are, however, partisan sentimentalism will continue to be widely prevalent, and
very powerful in defence of the spoils system.

All who labor for the removal of abuses are
sure to encounter a force which goes by the
name of

"BOURBONISM."

This is an unreasoning conservatism pro-
duced by a perversion of that attachment to
existing customs, relations and conditions,
which is designed to prevent hasty and injurious changes. It stands at the opposite extreme from that radicalism which is impatient
of all stability and takes no account of impossibilities. The Bourbon and the Radical alike,
are incapable of surveying the middle-ground
which lies between them; and each of them
classes with the other every person too
thoughtful to agree with him. The Radical
denounces the reformer as a Bourbon, while
the Bourbon sneers at him as a crack-brained

enthusiast. No man ever engaged in a reformatory enterprise without finding himself
violently opposed by those who have per-
versely allowed themselves to become incapable of apprehending the reasons for which
changes are demanded. On the strength of
their stolidity, they take to themselves the
credit of being eminently practical, and they
have only such names as "humbug," "fool"
and "crank," for those who are able to understand that many public evils are remediable.
The only curative treatment that can be recom-
mended, either to the Bourbon or to the Radical, is the cultivation of common sense. This
remedy having been duly applied, it will be
perceived, on the one hand, that many things
in this world ought to be conserved, and, on
the other, that occasional changes will be
needed until the millennium shall dawn.

The third element of the anti-reform spirit
is

CYNICISM.

Since I began writing this essay, it has oc-
curred to me very often that I am exposing
myself to a great deal of cynical contempt by

taking it for granted that a certain measure of moral decency should be observed in dealing with political matters. I have had conceptions of men speaking with curling lips and sniffing noses of "sermonizing on politics." Very well. If I could get the attention of the American voters who believe in the "sermonizing" that applies the rule of rectitude everywhere, I should ask no more. They form a class which is very apt to have its way in this country when a common impulse is alive among them.

The cynics of old seem to have limited themselves to a currish snarling at the more refined enjoyments, and the various arts and amenities of civilized life. But in the procession of the ages, all human aggregates designated by special names undergo important modifications. We find, accordingly, that the cynics of to-day bestow their snarling chiefly upon such aims and efforts as proceed from the more elevated impulses of man. Of course, the men who are working for the correction of abuses in the public service are called "good-goody politicians," and there is a great deal said about "Sunday-school statesmanship." Many other

expressions of the same order are in vogue,
all of them evincing a rankling bitterness toward those who act upon the principle that villainy in public affairs should not be tolerated.
It is easy enough for any one, who occupies a
moderately respectable moral plane, to look
down into these American cynics, and discover
what has happened to them. We have only
to remember how common it is for all honest
men to be denounced by knaves as hypocrites.
The experience of each one of us affords suffi-
ent data for the generalization : A human being is strongly inclined to maintain that no
other human being is better than himself. This
inclination is rendered measurably inoperative
in those who have learned the strength of their
perverse tendencies by struggling to overcome
them ; but it is apt to grow continually strong-
er in the absence of such efforts. It arises
from that principle in our nature, by reason of
which a consciousness of moral inferiority is
painful to us. It comes about, therefore, that
when we cannot keep our unworthiness from
flashing upon our intellectual vision, we have
a convulsive impulse to assert that we are as
good as anybody else, and that all who pro-

fess to be better than we know ourselves to
be are hypocrites ; and, if we happen to be sufficiently feeble-minded, we are able to per-
suade ourselves, for the moment, that the as-
sertion is true. But the most that the cynic
can do in this direction, does not suffice for
the extinguishment of the consciousness that
he is fooling himself in trying to maintain a
belief in his moral equality with decently fair-
minded men. Consequently, he experiences
a dissatisfaction for which he wants to punish
the persons with whom the comparison of himself is so irritating. It is in this way that his
malignant sneers, his scornful epithets, and
his contemptuous nicknames originate. The
human race will have to make great progress
before these causes of cynicism shall cease to
display their power wherever free institutions
invite the mass of citizens to political activity.
We must expect their violent opposition to
every change for the better in political methods, and in systems for the transaction of public business. There is some comfort, however, in the reflection that successful contests
with cynicism will promote the growth in
manly characteristics of those voters who de-

mand the exhibition in public life of some regard for what is morally becoming.

LOVE OF INTRIGUE.

For reasons which have momentous bearings
on human welfare, we are so constituted that
we take pleasure in the exercise of skill, as
well as in every other mode of personal efficiency.   This is one of the points in our
nature at which perversion is most common, and shows its worst results. Truman
Smith once said on the floor of the Senate:
"I have come to believe that, when a man
once gets it into his head that he is *cunning*,
there is no hope for him."   It is certain that
when a young man begins to plume himself on
his " smartness " in hoodwinking other men, or
in controlling their actions without giving them
a knowledge of his aims, he is in great danger
of becoming a false-hearted wretch. Like everything devilish, deceptive arts have a growing
fascination for those who tamper with them ;
and to this fact, undoubtedly, may be as-
cribed the entrance of multitudes of men on
criminal careers. Now, the spoils system
presents abundant opportunity for " working

in the dark,"—for plotting and contriving, with
a view to making the suffrages of the great
body of voters subservient to the personal ends
of the contriver. A score of different men
can be led to fix their hopes on a single
office, and thus to become, in their turn, secret
manipulators in the interest of the " boss " who
is misleading them. If this chieftain really has
great influence with the appointing power, or
if he can produce the impression that he has
extensive control in the distribution of offices,
he is able to have a little army of " workers "
at his command, and to chuckle over the skill
which he has exercised in organizing them, and
directing their movements. The most servile
and cunning of them are made recipients of the
official favors at his control, and the others are
persuaded that their turn will come very soon ;
or means for rewarding them pecuniarily are
raised by assessment of the more fortunate aspirants. In the meantime, all these workers—
the " appointed and the disappointed "—have
fallen under the fascinations of political intrigue, become averse to all respectable em-
ployments, and are now full-fledged professional politicians. " This is *politics !* " they and

their boss exclaim exultantly, whenever an especially villainous plot has been contrived. As
no man likes to see his occupation destroyed
and all opportunities for the exercise of his
skill abolished, and as all the hopes of "bosses"
and "workers" are inseparably connected with
the system which makes official position a reward of partisan service, it is to be expected
that all the powers at the command of those
who make a trade of the manipulation, or of
the acquisition, of such rewards, will be put
forth for the defeat of every measure designed
to raise the character of the public service.
The opportunities for intrigue, which attract
so many thousands to "practical politics," soon
come to be relied on exclusively for livelihood or advancement ; and all the voices of
selfishness cry out for the preservation of the
spoils system. Professional politicians will
clamor against reform as certainly as any evil
tree will bear evil fruit ; and they will have
the coöperation of all the amateurs in politics
who have acquired a taste for crooked practices.

The last element of the anti-reform spirit
which I shall name is

CONSCIOUSNESS OF INFERIORITY.

I have already pointed out the operation of this intellectual experience in the genesis of cynicism; but it has other effects of which we ought to take account. I do not say that, as a rule, spoilsmen admit, even to themselves, that they constitute a class of inferior men. Some of them are exceedingly egotistical, and habitually flatter themselves that there is something meritorious in the peculiar skill which they have acquired. But, after all, they know and feel that they are not qualified to achieve success in public life by the exhibition of fitness for the stations to which they aspire. They recognize the need of advantages external to their characters, and shrink from the prospect of competition on equal terms. The "bosses" have no confidence in their ability to over-match competitors in the display of states-manlike qualities, but see the danger of relega-tion to private life in everything that threatens them with deprivation of the control of patron-age. To partisan "workers" in the lower grades competitive examination is an ordeal not to be contemplated for a moment. They

know themselves to be destitute of qualifications for the public service; and the acquisition of fitness for good official work scarcely
occurs to them as a possible achievement.
Were these facts eliminated, the opposition to
reform in the Civil Service would lack much of
its present force.

It is but honest for me to call attention to
the fact that all these elements of the anti-reform spirit are entirely compatible with many
admirable personal qualities. Human nature
presents the possibility of very remarkable
combinations of good and evil. In a principal
spoilsman there is always something which at-
tracts the devoted attachment of subordinates.
He is often a man of lively sympathies and
disposed to be helpful with money and exertion. Within certain limits he may be called
honorable. It is not hard to find professional
politicians who obviously aim to be upright in
the ordinary affairs of life. That these men
are not altogether hateful is a source of gratification, though it has no connection with our
present subject. As voters, we are interested
simply in the characteristics which they display
in their endeavors to control the public busi-

ness; and when we see pernicious forces ema-
nating from them, our duty to our country
requires us to be resolute in supporting coun-
ter-active measures. I venture to hope, also,
that some of the young men inclined to political activity will find, in the analysis which I
have just concluded, good reasons for keeping
a watchful eye upon their own tendencies.

In advocating the prosecution of the reformatory work opposed by the elements of
force which I have pointed out, I cannot hope
to say much that is new. Some of the most
intellectual men of the age have discussed the
subject very thoroughly, and are discussing it
anew from day to day. But, aside from my
unwillingness to leave this essay incomplete, I
bear in mind the value of reiteration, and the
chance that one man's arguments may fall
under the notice of readers whom another's
have failed to reach. I will examine, in the
first place, some current

OBJECTIONS TO THE MERIT SYSTEM.

The purely sentimental objections have already received our attention; and I have
taken occasion, also, to notice the contempt

expressed in high places and in low places, for such statesmen as are disposed to put a reasonable restriction upon the demands of partisanship. There is so much of windy scoffing and of passionate clamor, on the part of those who oppose us in this matter, and they give us so little of what even bears the *form* of argumentation, that it is difficult to get at their intellectual standpoint. I will do my best, however, to make a fair statement of the positions which seem to me to have been taken.

1. *It is held that a government by the people should be administered through a political party, and that the merit system is incompatible with this theory.*

Instead of theorizing on the desirability of government by party, it is well for us to adjust ourselves to certain realities which we have no power to abolish. The forces of human nature make a contest between parties for the control of the government inevitable, except in such an "Era of good feeling," as that which followed the disappearance of the Federal party. But our national constitution, and the constitution of each state, make it possible for the executive branch to be controlled by

one party, while the legislative branch is under
the sway of another; and experience teaches
us that such conjunctures are by no means un-
common. Hence, our institutions do not assure so complete a government by party as
that which is witnessed in Great Britain,
where the administration must always be in
harmony with the majority the House of
Commons. Such completeness is liable, at
any time, to be precluded by the fundamental
principles of Republican government.

According to our constitution, and by reason
of the forces of human nature, a national contest is a struggle between parties for the *Head-
ship* of the executive branch of the government. It is true that, after the spoils system
came into existence, the scope of such contests
was extended to all the positions in the Civil
Service. But the constitution contains no
shadow of a provision for such extension; nor
was the scope of political contests so enlarged
while there were statesmen who had taken
part in the creation of our institutions. The
introduction of the spoils system was an inno-
vation upon the practices of those who founded
our government, and who may be supposed to

have known what was in harmony with its essential principles. They conferred upon the President authority to man the Civil Service, subject to restriction in the most important cases, through the confirming power of the Senate, which might or might not be in political harmony with him. The mere existence of that confirming power is utterly irreconcilable with the doctrine that the makers of the constitution contemplated the application of partisan tests in the appointment and retention of civil servants in general. If they had designed that all such servants of the people should be of the President's party, they would have made his appointing power absolute. They assumed, however, that he would recognize a momentous responsibility in connection with the transaction of the people's business, and apply only such tests as have a relation to faithfulness and efficiency.

Where there are clearly defined issues between the contending parties, it is right that the principles of the triumphant party should be carried out by the President whom it has elected, so far as that achievement is within the scope of his constitutional powers. To this end, his advisers and all his subordinates who have to do with the enforcement of the principles endorsed in his election, should be chosen from among the men who heartily accept those principles. It is right, too, that he should have officials of his own choosing, and in the fullest sympathy with him, sufficient in number for a survey of the service throughout its entire extent, and in all its ramifications. It is his duty thus to provide himself with all available information as to the need of changes in method or in the occupancy of positions. The advocates of the merit system concede these points without reserve, and would be ready to contend for them if they were assailed. But they regard the power of discrimination as a gift which has its uses; and they choose not to blind themselves to the boundaries within which the public welfare demands that the sway of party shall be confined. So far as the principles of the party controlling the administration can affect the character of the official work to be performed, the application of the partisan test is justifiable; but in favor of applying it beyond that limit, it is impossible for any man to frame an

argument entitled to be treated with respect.
Our constitution makes a complete government
by party, in the United States, a matter of
only occasional possibility ; and Great Britain
has demonstrated that the completest government by party in the world is entirely compatible with an exceedingly limited application of
the partisan test.

2. *It is maintained that the will of the people
is defeated when opponents of the dominant party
are employed in the Civil Service.*

I suppose that there is as much meaningless
verbiage gathered around what is called " The
will of the people," as it is possible to find
in any other connection, and that no other subject surpasses this in affording material for
demagogic harangues.   It is observed that the
popular will is uniformly held to be the will of
a majority at a given election, though it may
be a majority of one in a total vote of a million.
The minority, however large, is treated as having no part in the manifestation of the will of
the people, and as having no right to an influence in the administration of the government.
This is alleged to be justified on the ground
that, under Republican institutions, the wishes

of a majority of voters are necessarily taken to be identical with the wishes of the whole people. But is that true? In one instance, at least, the popular majority was against the candidate who was elected to the Presidency, and such may be the result of any contest for that office. There is no certainty that either House of Congress will be controlled by the party which has a majority of the popular vote. It is said that one of the parties in the State of New York must have a majority of thirty thousand or more, in order to be assured of legislative control. It follows from the very nature of our institutions that the popular minority is sure to be largely influential in shaping the legislation of the country; and this we know to have been especially designed by the authors of the Federal constitution. The merit system, duly extended, would simply bring the executive department of the government into conformity with the legislative department, by opening the way for the participation of minorities. So far as the spoils system is in force, the general spirit of our institutions is thwarted, and the form of our government is made grossly unsymmetrical.

If the political affiliations of civil servants were of any importance, and if it were necessary to talk about the "will of the people" in the matter, a little exercise of common sense would bring us to the conclusion that the offices ought to be divided between the parties. There is nothing bearing the semblance of justification for the view, that the wishes of one-half the voters should be utterly ignored, and that those of the other half should be treated as the wishes of the whole people. But suppose we set aside all that I have heretofore said, and admit that the party which succeeds in electing a President has a right to make its own will stand for the will of the American people. We now have before us such questions as these: Did that party, on the day of election, pronounce in favor of excluding from the Civil Service all members of the opposite party? Was such action commended in its platform? Was a purpose to secure such exclusion indicated in the character and record of its candidate? No well-informed person is ignorant of the fact that, at any time since the merit system began to be advocated in this country, a frank avowal in favor of the spoils system, by either of the parties at a national convention, would have been followed by that party's overwhelming defeat. No party will ever dare to place itself before the people on a platform containing that avowal. When the spoils-mongers, professional politicians and servile partisans assume to speak for their respective parties, they exaggerate their own importance preposterously; and when those of them who belong to the party controlling the administration, pretend on the strength of that ascendancy, to voice the will of the American people, their impudence takes on colossal proportions.

3. *We are told that the merit system infringes the common right of American citizens to employment in the public service.*

I have credited myself with some little skill in conjecturing what might be said in opposition to my views; but I confess that I should not have hit upon this objection if I had neither heard nor read a statement of it. A citizen has the same right to a position in the Civil Service that he has to be elected to Congress, or to get rich. This falls under the general right to "the pursuit of happiness;" and the enforcement of it depends partly on personal characteristics, and partly on external circumstances. This political right, however, is not absolute. The several states have power to modify it by establishing pre-requisites to the privilege of voting and conditions of eligibility; and the Federal Government has ample authority to prescribe qualifications for positions in the Civil Service. It is self-evident that no man has a right to a public position for which he is incompetent, and, therefore, that no man's right can be infringed by the requirement of competency. But there is something else to be said upon this matter. Every citizen has a right to demand that, in the ascertainment of his qualifications, no unreasonable test shall be applied, and that he shall not be placed at a disadvantage relatively to any class of his fellow-citizens. The securing of this right to all American citizens is of the very essence of the merit system; while the spoils system, in barring out from the Civil Service nearly one-half of the population of the United States, is diametrically antagonistic to the political equality of which we boast. Any governmental discrimination, which deprives merit of its reward is an infringement upon personal rights.

4. *It is held that the existence of a permanent office-holding class is contrary to the spirit of free institutions.*

This objection, at the first glance, appears to have some force; and I suppose it is now causing hesitation on the part of many thoughtful and patriotic men. It seems to me that the radical error lies in a false conception of the nature of the Civil Service, and in the consequent imagination of an analogy which does not exist. Because the civil servants are employed in the business of the government, they are supposed to exercise a governing power; and it is assumed that, if they were to hold their positions permanently, their case would be analogous to that of hereditary participants in goverment under monarchial institutions. There is no ground for this view. None of the officials, to whom the most advanced reformers would have the merit system extended, can be said with any propriety to constitute a part of the government. None of them are clothed with even the slightest authority to exert an influence upon the making of laws, or upon the policy of the administration. On the contrary, they are placed under restrictions from which other citizens are exempt. Americans not connected with the public service have an unlimited right to devote time and labor, with a view to the assurance of such a governmental policy as will accord with their desires. But the spirit of the merit system requires the confinement of such activity, on the part of civil servants, within very narrow bounds. Instead of having official power to take part in determining the policy of the government, and the occupancy of its chief positions, the merit system would subject them to a special disability as to the exercise of such influence. If *ruling* differs from *serving*, none of the valid objections to a permanent governing class can apply to a body of civil servants holding their positions during good behavior. It should be remembered, also, that none of the reformers desire to deprive appointing officers of the power of removal. So far as that matter is concerned, they are laboring simply to create a public opinion which shall condemn the exercise of that power for reasons having no relation to the good of the service.

Some persons evidently regard employment in the Civil Service as the enjoyment of a valuable privilege, and consequently hold that there should be rotation in it. Permanency of tenure appears to them in the light of monopoly. This, too, is an erroneous conception. Many of our most intelligent citizens are of the opinion that comparatively few honest civil servants have advanced their personal fortunes as rapidly as they might have done in private life. The advocates of the merit system are very earnest in demanding that compensation for public service shall be no greater than that which is paid for private service requiring similar efficiency and trustworthiness; and they will always insist that public life shall present no exceptional opportunities for the accumulation of wealth. There is nothing in this objection which should have a particle of force in moving the fifty-five millions of our people to forego the benefits of experience in the transaction of their business; and nothing can be said in opposition to tenure during good behavior in the subordinate Civil Service, which could not be alleged with equal reason against permanency of identification with any other

calling. The spirit of our institutions is an-
tagonized by the merit system no more than
it is by the employment of the same men for
a long term of years in the service of a railroad company. Other considerations, which
would be pertinent here, will be presented in
connection with the fruits of the spoils system.

5. *Some men frankly avow their acceptance of
the maxim : " To the victors belong the spoils,"
and base their opposition to the merit system on
that ground.*

The metaphorical phraseology of this maxim is derived from a mode of warfare which is
no longer tolerated among civilized nations.
When war was waged for plunder, and no
moral obligation was recognized, the victorious hordes found compensation for service in
the possession of " spoils." The maxim, in
its literal sense, is distinctively barbarian, and
the sentiment which it is now employed to express is thoroughly atrocious. It grew out of
the conception of a contest between parties
as nothing higher than a savage scramble for
official positions; and it embodies the assumption that none but office-holders and office-
seekers are interested in the results of elec-

tions. It presents voters in general as the brainless tools of spoilsmen. To be sure, the maxim is sometimes thoughtlessly commended by men of fair intelligence against whom nothing worse than partisan servility can be alleged. If such men, however, would take a little time for reflection, they would see that no step can be taken in the direction of treating official positions as "spoils," without detriment to the public welfare, and that nothing can "belong" to a victorious party except opportunities to advance that welfare. Places in the Civil Service exist for the benefit of the whole people, and not for the benefit of an insignificant number of men who may happen to be identified with the party which succeeds in gaining control of a single department of the government; and any diversion of care from the former end to the latter is necessarily unpatriotic.

In discussing

THE FRUITS OF THE SPOILS SYSTEM,

I shall figure it to myself in its completeness —as it existed before the enactment of what is known as the Civil Service law. This I think to be proper, because the advocates of the system are unanimous in denouncing the law, and manifest a desire for its repeal which nothing but the fear of the people keeps them from openly avowing. If they should ever be triumphant in a national contest, they would, at least, secure such evasions of the law by appointing officers as would amount to the practical nullification of it, and the case of the Civil Service would then be like that of the man into whom the seven devils re-entered, with seven other devils worse than themselves. A triumphant reaction is likely to go beyond the point at which the reformatory action commenced; and when officials are induced to evade the laws which they are sworn to enforce, they are inspired with a taste for villainy to which no bounds can be set.

To residents of rural districts, where postmasters are the only Federal officials, no great evil resulting from the spoils system may have been apparent. They should remember, however, that the important national business is transacted at the seat of government and in the large cities, where such officials are numerous. I will ask them, also, to trace the causes, which I shall point out, to their inevitable effects, and to bear in mind the testimony which has been given by men who have observed the operation of those causes.

The spoils system is the same in its nature and in its practical working wherever it is applied. As a matter of convenience, I shall speak of it only in its relation to the business of the general Government ; but all will understand, of course, that it is equally pernicious when applied to the business of a State or to that of a city. In fact, its worst results have been witnessed in connection with municipal affairs. I hold that the merit system should be enforced wherever public business is to be transacted by appointed officials. I now ask attention to the following specifications :

1. *Taxation of the People for the Benefit of Spoilsmen.*

All unnecessary expenditures in the administration of the Government involve the necessity of unjust taxation. All the cost of the Civil Service, in excess of a fair compensation to competent officials, giving undivided attention to the duties of their respective positions, with proper facilities and materials, is a burden

wrongfully imposed upon the people. But
under the spoils system these circumstances
are observed : In the first place, thousands of
incompetent men are brought into the service.
They receive their positions as rewards for
partisan exertion, or as remuneration for servility to leading spoilsmen. From the mere
fact that they have devoted themselves to the
work for which they receive these political rewards, it is reasonable to infer that they lack
those characteristics which make men efficient
and successful in the business of private life.
They have failed to obtain employment from
those sagacious men of affairs, who are always on the watch for trustworthy men ; and
the service which they have been rendering has
tended to aggravate their unfitness for the con-
fining and laborious duties of their official positions. Now, no intelligent man needs to have
his attention drawn to the difference between
the cost of a given amount of work accomplished through good service, and that of the
same amount accomplished through poor service. It often occurs that all the difference
between a profitable business and a losing
business is created by the selection of sub-

ordinates who can be relied on to work both swiftly and thoroughly. A superintendent who is negligent in the manning of responsible positions will wreck an enterprise, while one who uses due diligence in the matter will conduct it to a triumphant success. In a case of the former kind, work is performed slowly, and much time must be taken up in the rectification of blunders. Consequently, the number of persons employed and the aggregate of salaries paid, are often in such excess over what they would have been if subordinates had been wisely chosen, as to sweep away all profits. Besides, when the details of a large business are in the hands of incompetent men, there are always losses on the right hand and on the left, and there is a continual presentation of opportunities for stealing with little apparent danger of detection. Of course these considerations apply to the public business as fully as to the business of a private firm, or to that of a corporation.

But the spoils system does not permit the civil servants to devote to their official duties all the labor for which they are paid with money derived from taxation of the people. It requires them, in consideration of their retention in office, to set apart much of their time for partisan work. It treats many offices, to which large salaries are attached, as purely political, providing for the transaction of all the official business by deputies and other subordinates, and setting the nominal incumbents free to devote themselves exclusively to partisan work in the interests of their respective chieftains. To pay for all this partisan work demanded of civil servants, under the spoils system, all the people are taxed, though a majority of them may be politically hostile to the spoilsmen who receive their money.

There is still another point to be considered here. The spoils system requires that the members of the Civil Service shall be overpaid to such an extent—that they shall find it for their interest to purchase the privilege of continuing in office by submitting to heavy assessments for the benefit of the party controlling the administration. A due consideration of these points cannot fail to convince a thoughful person that the spoils system makes the cost of the Civil Service greater, by many millions annually, than it ought to be. For that excess of cost all the people are taxed ; and the sole benefit accrues to the spoilsmen who traffic in places of trust for selfish ends.

2. *Ignoring of proved Efficiency and Trust-worthiness.*

I have had occasion to remember a thousand times a circumstance which fell under my notice many years ago. The managing partner in a commercial establishment consulted a non-resident partner as to the retention of an employee, who had determined to work no longer on a simple salary. The answer was in these words : " Sell Russell an interest on his own terms, if that is the only way to retain him ; for I tell you good men are scarce." It may be that " good men " have become more numerous since that time ; and I am inclined to believe that an employer who seeks them with sufficient earnestness can always find enough of them to fill the places at his control. Still, in every service except that of the Government the unnecessary dismissal of a tried and trusted employee, who had thoroughly familiarized himself with the intricate duties of a responsible position, would be regarded by all intelligent business men as an act of egregious stupidity. Let the executive head of a corporation be known to have committed a few such blunders as that, and then let him hear what his directors and stockholders have to say. But the upholders of the spoils system cry out for a "clean sweep" at every transfer of the chief administrative power from one party to another. All demonstrated elements of efficiency, all well-earned titles to perfect trust, and all the fitness derived from experience, are to count for nothing; and untried men, with no knowledge of the duties to which they are called, are to take possession of the Civil Service throughout its entire extent. I have never heard of a man foolish enough to conduct his private business in that way, and I find it hard to be patient with those who favor the injection of such foolishness into the management of the people's business.

3. *Application of tests condemned by common-sense.*

I am glad to be able to say that some appointing officers conscientiously endeavor to couple the test of fitness with the partisan test. It is true, too, that many Senators and

Representatives in Congress, in recommending appointments, aim to select competent persons from among their political friends. Still, there is an obvious and a very serious disadvantage in the narrowing of the field of choice to the limits of a single party. No prudent manager, charged with the manning of a great establishment, and intent on securing the best service possible, would consent to be confined in his choice of assistants to the members of his own political party, any more than he would cripple himself by determining to employ only blue-eyed men. Insisting upon requirements which have no pertinency to the case in hand, is always contrary to the dictates of practical wisdom. But the partisan test is not the only irrelevant test of which the application is made certain by the spoils system. In myriads of cases, if not as a rule, the test of loyalty to a particular leader is enforced with equal strictness, and thus the field of choice is made still narrower. In a given locality there may be competent aspirants enough among the adherents of the party controlling the executive branch of the government, while it may be very hard to find such aspirants among

the devoted followers of the leader most influential with appointing officers. Devotion to
the political fortunes of an ambitious chieftain,
comes very far short of indicating fitness for
official work. It is by no means prophetic of
patient industry and careful guardianship of
the public interests. To make the matter
worse, all the selfish impulses of the patron
impel him to treat serviceableness to himself
as the supreme qualifications for the offices at
his disposal ; and he is in danger, when making his recommendations, of utterly failing to
take into account the probability or improba-
bility of good official work.

These tests are condemned by common-
sense, not only because they stand in the way
of a judicious manning of the Civil Service, but
because, also, they are palpably unjust. Any
American citizen has a right to complain when
employment is made impossible to him on
grounds which have no relation to his qualifications for it. No one, at this day, would
attempt to justify the religious tests formerly
enforced in Great Britain. But what can be
said against the governmental disqualification
of Jews or Roman Catholics, that cannot be

urged with equal reason against the exclusion of Democrats or Republicans from positions on the duties of which their political principles have no possible bearing? This is not the whole case. The spoils system, as I have shown, brings into force the test of adhesion to some political chief. Is there justice to American citizens in general, when the absence of a personal relation of that kind is made a disqualification for public employment? Is it just to lay down the rule, that Americans must either cease to think and act with manly independence, or renounce all hopes of appointment to the Civil Service?

4. *Degradation of Politics.*

I have argued on former pages in favor of an operative interest in all the political movements which are believed to promise benefit to our country. Politics, in my view, should be a matter of deep concern to each one of us. The abstention of a large part of our voting population from political activity is inconsistent with the theory of Government by the People. According to that theory, the voter is to inform himself of the public needs, and to satisfy himself as to the measures which will be best for the country; and then by appealing to the understandings and patriotic impulses of his fellow-voters, he is to labor for the adoption and carrying into effect of those measures through the agency of persons whom his support shall help to clothe with the requisite authority. To do this, is to engage in the legitimate politics of a Republic ; and politics thus viewed, is fruitful of ennobling influences. In so far as political activity is governed by lower aims, with selfishness taking the place of patriotism, we witness the degradation which I have specified.

No one claims that the annihilation of the spoils system would assure us all we need in the way of political purification. I have already pointed out the debasing influences of partisan servility; and it is easy to see that other vices will continue to make their power felt in the treatment of public affairs. Nevertheless, the merit system, duly extended and rigidly enforced, would go far in the direction of precluding the operation of those vices in connection with the politics of the country. Consider, in the first place, how party spirit is made passionate, unreasoning and unscrupulous. It is in the nature of this affection, when grown into a passion, to make the prospect of gain and the possibility of loss, to one's party, quite as powerful in stimulating to exertion and in smothering scruples as they would be if only the partisan's individual interests were in question. But the spoils system puts forward more than a hundred thousand offices, with emoluments, to be counted by hundreds of millions, as a prize to be won or lost in a contest between parties for the control of the national administration. We are all familiar with the consequences. To millions of voters bare success becomes the end to which all considerations of patriotism and moral decency are subordinated. They demand that no question but that of availability shall be entertained in the nomination of candidates, and that platforms shall be framed with an eye single to the winning of votes. They insist that their national conventions shall furnish materials with which they may pander to special animosities, and appeal to the selfishness of the various classes that are demanding special benefits through governmental action. And these frenzied clamorers are very apt to have their way.

Their impulses have a vehemence which gives
them an easy victory over their more considerate
fellow-partisans. As the canvass progresses,
the offices and their emoluments take on more
maddening attractions, and the feeling that
they must be possessed at all hazards, grows
more intense and becomes more pervasive.
Men, who are capable of high statesmanship
and have deserved well of their country in
many things, are infected with the rage for
spoils, and are not ashamed to go before the
people with appeals to evil passion, and with
sophistical arguments which a school-boy could
tear into shreds. Then come assessments of
office-holders on the one side and of office-
seekers on the other; obtaining of huge con-
tributions by promises of governmental favor
and pictures of overwhelming ruin; levying of
black-mail in consideration of immunity for
official villainy, and appeals to all servile partisans for their last dollar. The millions thus
accumulated are disbursed by agents selected
for their unscrupulousness and their proficiency
in all the modes of corruption; and money is
made to flow in steady streams to the states in
which purchaseable voters are supposed to

hold the balance of power. How does this compare with the politics provided for in the true theory of government by the people? It is true that a perverted party spirit, even in the absence of such a prize as the Civil Service, may be expected to impel men to some excesses. But no man can mentally eliminate the influences flowing from the spoils system and then see, in the remaining forces, a potentiality sufficient to account for anything resembling the disgraceful partisan warfare which we have witnessed in recent years. It is only when party spirit is wholly dissevered from patriotism and swallowed up by an unmitigated thirst for official emoluments, that it can become a maddening passion regardless of moral principle.

Still grosser impulses are brought into play by the seductions of a partisan Civil Service. Zeal for party is re-enforced by personal greed ; and the victory of party comes to be regarded simply as a pre-requisite to the triumph of selfishness. The men, who are thus moved to political activity by a craving for support at the public expense, may be numbered by the hundred thousand ; and, considering the demoralization which has already resulted from passionate partisanship, it is hard to name a limit beyond which this new force will not carry them. There are honorable exceptions, of course; and yet it remains true that, in almost every community during a national contest, there are aspirants to positions in the Civil Service who accept in its fullness the maxim: "All is fair in politics." Having staked all their hopes on the results of the conflict, it is to be expected that their villainous practices will be commensurate with their opportunities. It is needless to dwell on the alliances between these men and the candidates for elective offices who are expected to be influential as to the distribution of spoils, or to speak at length on their persistency and skill in controlling caucuses and conventions. It is enough to know that they are always at the front in politics, and that they touch nothing which they do not defile.

I have not yet spoken of the most odious feature of this degradation. After the strife between parties is ended, the spoilsmen of the victorious party turn their weapons upon each other. "Boss" wages war upon "boss," and faction arrays itself against faction. The rage for spoils is manifesting itself everywhere. There is a separate battle over each position that is to be filled; and, throughout the land, there is an engendering of enmities which will last for years. In what direction these things tend, was illustrated a few years ago in a way which no American should ever forget. A change in the occupancy of an important post was made with a view to the acquisition of control, in a great State, over the machinery of the dominant party. We all remember what passions were inflamed and what madness filled the air. The assassination of Garfield was the world-horrifying fruit of that war between factions over the political power which the spoils system attaches to control of positions in the Civil Service. How fully the men who object to a system which invites such conflicts deserve to be sneered at as "Goody-goody politicians!" What good reason men, who might be statesmen, have for denouncing as a "pretentious humbug" the system which would shut out from the field of American politics all the iniquities evoked by a partisan Civil Service, and would destroy forever the occupation of the professional spoilsman!

5. *Prevention of Patriotic Exertion.*

It is sufficient in this place merely to remind the reader of what has been said on former pages concerning the disrepute thrown upon partisan activity by the conspicuousness of base men, and by the consequent introduction of disgraceful practices. Thus it has come about that personal degradation is insepar-ably joined, in the conceptions of many self-respecting men, with activity in politics, and that multitudes of our best citizens are kept aloof from the movements preliminary to political contests. I have stated the convic-tion, that patriotic citizens ought to over-come their repugnance to contact with the men known as " workers," and ought to par-ticipate actively in all the proceedings which have a determining influence on the characters and attitudes of their respective parties. But the unquestionable fact remains that, in propor-tion as men of low character shall be attracted to politics by rewards to sordid selfishness, men of high character will be caused to repress their patriotic impulses. Now, let the reader im-agine the Civil Service thoroughly non-partisan, and all appointing power regulated in accordanee with the merit system, and then let him seek for the remaining inducements to conspicuous intermeddling with politics on the part of characterless "workers." As a class, they would disappear from the field of political action; and the strongest barrier to patriotic exertion by enlightened citizens would be broken down.

6. *Fostering of Oligarchical Power.*

There is but one step between predominance in directing the action of a national party and predominance in the administration of the Government. That step is taken when a party becomes completely triumphant. Hence, a large measure of governmental power proceeds from the body of leaders who control the nominations, and adjust the aims, of the party destined to be successful, whatever their nominal positions may be. There is nothing to be deplored in the mere certainty that, under Republican institutions, there will always be a class of men exceptionally powerful in shaping the characters of parties, and, consequently, in determining governmental action. If they are *deservedly* powerful, their existence is an immense boon to their country. The influence

which men acquire by wisdom, integrity and
persevering labor for the public good, is always
beneficent, and the growth of it is full of
promise for the people. But the case is very
different when power is built up by intrigue
and through alliances based on a common selfishness. The spirit in which such power will
be employed is sure to be in keeping with the
baseness of its origin; and no ascent by tortu-
ous paths, to leadership in a party destined to
control the Government, can fail to be detri-
mental to the country. The interests of the
people demand the sweeping away, so far as is
possible, of all instrumentalities for the build-
ing-up of political power having no basis in
personal merits. But the spoils system furnishes the ambitious schemer for ascendancy
in his party with nearly all his stock in trade.
He attaches men to his political· fortunes by
promising positions in the Civil Service ; and
the extent of his following, thus secured, is
measured solely by the estimate that is placed
on his ability to fulfill such promises. In proportion as he is able to increase the number of
his servile adherents, and to direct their movements cunningly, his friendship is considered

valuable by appointing officers, and his control
over the disposition of places is extended. To
strengthen himself by the bestowal of patronage is to strengthen himself for grasping
more patronage to be used in the same way.
Through such processes a class of mighty
"bosses" comes into existence, with a power
essentially oligarchical and thoroughly antagonistic to the spirit of free institutions. Instances of rise to enormous domination, by
skill and perseverance in manipulating the instrumentalities afforded by the spoils system,
will occur to every reader. We have seen
leaders so extending and invigorating their
sway through the efficacy of spoils, that the
conventions of their party, in their respective
States, have submitted to their dictation
unquestioningly through successive years.
Smaller "bosses," with more restricted spheres,
have been dictating nominations and pre-
determining the results of elections wherever
numerous offices are filled by appointment.
It is obvious that a partisan Civil Service is
entirely out of place under a constitution providing for popular self-government. We ought
to remember, also, that the selfish ends, which

were paramount in the acquisition of oligarchical power, are sure to be kept paramount in
the employment of it.

7. *Excitement of Injurious Hopes.*

This may seem to be an unimportant point,
but nothing, connected with governmental
action and affecting the happiness of many
citizens, should be disregarded by those who
desire to have public affairs administered beneficently. Let us suppose the completeness
of the spoils system restored by a repeal of
the present statute, or by such an official nullification of it, and such a total abrogation of its
spirit as would result from a national triumph
of spoilsmen. We know that what sagacious
men view as the barest possibility of defeating
the party in control of the Administration, is
regarded as almost a certainty by the more
sanguine members of the opposition. Hence,
no sooner does a national canvass begin to wax
hot, than a multitude of partisans, outnum-
bering many times the places to be filled by
appointment, begin to entertain strong hopes
of sharing in the spoils to be distributed in the
event of their party's success. They drop all
plans for gaining livelihood in private occupa-

tions, and neglect their work in hand, in order to establish titles to positions in the Civil Service by conspicuous partisanship. Even if a transfer of administrative power is brought about, four-fifths of these men, at least, are necessarily disappointed, because there is a limit beyond which needless positions in the service cannot be multiplied. Chagrin and bitterness are felt; embarrassments, resulting from waste of time and neglect of opportunities, must be struggled with; there is an abatement of inclination to ordinary vocations, and, worst of all, a sad deterioration of character is apt to result. When we consider that the men who share in these experiences are to be counted by hundreds of thousands, we are compelled to see that the aggregate evil, accruing from this fruit of the spoils system, is immense.

8. *Debasement of Ideals.*

Every man, sufficiently developed to feel a lively interest in the qualities of his own personality, has a conception of his future self and aspires to the realization of it. The characteristics of this ideal are immeasurably important, because the downward gravitation of man makes it certain that he will prove less worthy

than he aims to be. Every man comes short
of his intended measure of self-coercion; and
if his ideal is low, his personality will be still
more degraded. While these conceptions of
future selves are growing into form in the
minds of young men, they almost invariably at-
tach undue importance to what the world calls
success, and become unduly desirous of making
it their own. It is thus that they arrive at the
perverse treatment of their personalities as
means to external ends, and thus that the qualities which they deem pre-requisite to successful achievement enter too largely into their
ideals. They derive their view of the nature
of those qualities from what they observe in
those who are most efficient in bringing about
the results at which they aim; and, in a country
where political success is very generally over-
valued, it is natural that their attention should
be directed largely to the men whom they may
see to be successful in political management.
In this way they come to view the qualities of
influential spoilsmen with complacency; they
see something admirable in effective chicanery,
and a bewitching freedom from restraint in unscrupulousness. Then the fascinations of in-

trigue, which I have heretofore pointed out, lay hold upon them, and all the falseness and meanness belonging to a miserable cunning are incorporated in their ideals. Reflection upon this subject conducts us irresistibly to the conclusion that, within the last fifty years, the influences of the spoils system have proved mighty for degradation of character, through debasement of ideals, to millions of our fellow-citizens. Let us remember here that the elevation of Americans is the highest end of American patriotism, and that their demoralization is the worst evil that can befall our country.

9. *Disabling of Legislators and Appointing Officers.*

This effect, if it stood alone, would amply warrant the condemnation of the spoils system. For a long time after the transfer of chief administrative power from one party to another, or from one faction to another, the members of the new administration are subjected to a crushing pressure by importunities for appointment. At the very time when they most need to be unembarrassed, in order that they may familiarize themselves with their new duties, it is scarcely possible for them to seize upon two consecutive hours for the uninterrupted pursuit of their legitimate work. Even with the immense relief afforded by the Civil Service law, it was many months from the accession of the present administration before the pressure for office had perceptibly abated ; and, all the while, the interests of fifty-five millions were suffering in order that place-hunters and their patrons might be treated respectfully. Under such circumstances, the commission of many errors; the postponement of needed action, and delay in systematizing official work, are inevitable. With the spoils system fully re-established, the clamor for office would interfere continually with the transaction of public business. Even now, officials vested with appointing power find no period of entire freedom from such embarrassment. An indestructible determination to secure official employment seems to be widely prevalent, and to be associated with a total incapacity for the recognition of impossibilities.

If we turn now to the Congressional patrons of applicants for position in the Civil Service, we have the testimony of Democratic Senators and Representatives to the effect that, during the recent protracted session, they had absolutely no time for a satisfactory investigation of the important subjects on which they were required to take action. There were letters to be answered, petitions to be considered, conflicting claims to be weighed, the value of support to be compared with the cost of enmity and numberless interviews to be held with appointing officers. It is plain that the perplexities connected with these proceedings, and the disgust occasioned by the necessity of them, are far from being favorable to patient and fruitful study. To be sure, there are some Congressmen who enjoy such work, and build all their hopes on proficiency in it; and I admit that, so far as men of that class have their time thus pre-occupied, there is little loss to the country, because they cannot, in any event, be expected to understand the bearings of proposed measures. But there are many other Senators and Representatives who honestly desire to render good service, and who have such powers that their deliverance from the crippling influences of the spoils system would redound immensely to the public benefit.

I have the impression that we are very prone to underestimate the importance of unrestricted opportunity for intellectual labor on the part of those who make and those who execute our laws. Without resolute and long-continued meditation, we can obtain no adequate view of the weightiness and complexity of the matters with which they are called upon to deal. Moreover our fortunate experiences have led us to flatter ourselves that no blundering in legislation and no mis-management in administration can seriously interrupt our national prosperity. This I believe to be a terrible mistake. No man has higher hopes than I have as to the future of the United States; but all my confidence is based on the assumption that able men, working energetically and without impediment, will bring the wonder-working power of thought to bear upon our public affairs. Since I began to reflect on these things I have come in view of subjects so complicated, and having such momentous relations to the welfare of our people, that I have experienced genuine satisfaction every day in reflecting that I have only the responsibility of a private citizen in connection with them. The possibility of a disastrous crisis is always present ; and safeguards against such events are always needed. I see great difficulties in the indisputable reality, that we must either make ourselves able to place manufactured articles on sale at a lower cost, or abandon all hope of successful competition with other nations in the markets of the world, so far as the products of manufacturing industry are concerned; and I recognize the need of an exhaustive forethinking of consequences in connection with each alternative. I am unprepared to say how far the state of things, in those countries with which we have extensive commercial relations, should be taken into account while we are devising measures for the regulation of our own circulating medium. I do not perceive distinctly how equal justice can be assured to the debtors and the creditors of the land, though I am confident that we have statesmen with brain-power enough for the solution of the problem, if they can be permitted to use it. I am unable to make a statement, satisfactory to myself, of considerations for and against a resolute and systematic endeavor to regain a reasonable share in the carrying trade on the high seas. Other and still more momentous questions are emerging,—questions growing out of the rapid increase of our population, the rapid diminution of our unoccupied territory, the enormous advance in the use of labor-saving machinery and the immigration of reckless agitators and disciples of agitators. Down to this time, our legislators have given us little upon these questions, beyond vote-catching claptrap and manifestations of vote-regarding cowardice. In the meantime, portentous embodiments of force are growing up, and putting forth menaces which justify most appalling visions of what the future may have in store for us. In relation to these matters my own mind is clear only on the single fact that, sooner or later, these tremendous forces must be subjected to governmental regulation. To leave unrestricted a power by which a single individual, or a central committee, can command the unhesitating obedience of myriads, and throw the business of a vast region into disorder, is of the very essence of anarchy. I am not competent to devise the requisite measures; but, as I believe in the possibility of salvation, I believe that a system of legislative provisions, assuring the preservation of order and the equable flow of industry, and bringing the interests of wages-earners into perfect harmony with the interests of employers, is within the reach of patriotic statesmanship.

Under the best system that is possible, there will always be enough of intellectual flippancy, and an over-supply of those men who credit themselves with the full mastery of a subject as soon as they have caught a partial glimpse of its surface. Because such persons are sure to be putting forward their crudities, there is all the more need of perfect freedom for intellectual exertion by those who are capable of comprehending the limitations of their knowledge, and are disposed to work for its enlargement. In view of all the subjects fraught with such unspeakable moment to the American people, and calling so imperatively for the uninterrupted application of the best intellects, it seems to me but little less than treasonable to maintain a system which throws upon our national legislators, and chief administrative officers, the miserable, time-consuming and mind-unhinging annoyances connected with the impossible task of satisfying ever-obtruding throngs of importunate place-hunters. The spoils system is altogether damnable.

CONCLUSION.

I have written the foregoing pages with a desire to contribute the little in my power to the awakening of thought on the part of such of my fellow-citizens as are able to "render a reason" for political action, and have no wish pertaining to the Government except that it be wisely and righteously administered. Subject only to the determinations of Providence, the men of that class are able to control the destinies of this country. By virtue of their numbers, and through the might of intelligence, they can make demagogues powerless, keep the incompetent in private life, utterly crush all organizers of corruption, and secure to us the services of able and patriotic statesmen completely free from all that would impede them in arriving at an understanding of what is best for us. Believing that the patriotism of such American citizens will be increasingly vigorous and thoughtful, I feel assured that it will be well with our country in the coming ages.